Run to the Waterfall

Run to the Waterfall

by

Arturo Vivante

CHARLES SCRIBNER'S SONS

Copyright © 1962, 1964, 1966, 1967, 1968, 1970, 1972, 1973, 1974, 1975, 1976, 1977, 1979 Arturo Vivante

Library of Congress Cataloging in Publication Data

Vivante, Arturo.
Run to the waterfall.

I. Title.
PZ4.V85Ru   [PS3572.I85]   813'.5'4   79–15448
ISBN 0–684–16276–8

All of the stories in this collection appeared originally in *The New Yorker*.

This book published simultaneously in the United States of America and Canada.

1 3 5 7 9 11 13 15 17 19 O/C 20 18 16 14 12 10 8 6 4 2

To my mother and father

Contents

Run to the Waterfall

A Game of
Light and Shade

THERE was a time, before the conquerors came and razed them nearly all, when Siena had a skyline thick with towers. The steeple of the cathedral and the bell towers of the churches were left standing, and one other —the highest and the oldest, the tower of the town hall. It stems from the left corner of the communal palace and rises more than three hundred feet over the piazza. It stands erect. It is so old, so tall, it can't afford to lean. Especially if you look at it from below, you wonder how in the fourteenth century anyone dared build anything so high.

Visitors may climb to the top. A little door at the foot of the tower, in the courtyard of the town hall, opens into a small, zigzagging stone stairway. A short distance up, a passage leads from it into the palace and the ticket office. You go up a flight of steps to a terrace, where a door brings you back into the zigzagging stairway of the tower. Here there is even less room than below, and you hope you won't meet someone coming down. The walls are so thick and the space so scanty you feel you are inside the hollow core of a great tree. The stairway widens somewhat farther up. It changes as you climb. No step is like the next one. Only the thickness of the walls, seen through narrow openings that show the sky, seems constant. Within them you feel secure.

The tower was begun in 1325 and raised as the commune grew bolder. In 1345, at the peak of its glory, the tower reached its present height. From the piazza, if you look closely, you may see, marked by a slight but abrupt change in the color of the bricks, the outlines of former stages.

The stairs zigzag around a hollow shaft. This is the very core, the pith, of the tower. Through it run two big ropes, used to ring the bells that hang in the turret above. With them, in an emergency, the government of Siena could put the whole town and the countryside around it in a state of alarm. I've often heard their plangent, deep, dramatic tone, and almost felt the waves of sound. In Fascist times, they used to be rung whenever there was a parade. The sound carried me centuries back to when it meant something and didn't just strike a hollow and empty note.

Slits in the walls, and at intervals narrow, tall windows with a pointed arch, bring air and light. Most other towers have dark, monotonous stairways that make you despair of ever coming to the top. Here, instead, you reach it sooner than you think.

The red bricks of the stem blossom into travertine, white machicolations, and the stairway opens onto a crenellated terrace. There is a view of hills and mountains, of the cathedral and the roofs of the town. If you lean over the crenels on one side, you see the red brick square below, radiated like an open fan.

A tall, arched stone bell tower rises from the terrace. You may climb this, too, past the bells it lodges, to a second terrace, and go still higher, up to a platform that supports a weather vane and yet another bell.

I have climbed the tower twice in my life—the first time in my childhood, the second recently. I should really say that I've been up three times, for when I recently climbed it something happened that made me go up again as soon as I had come down.

It was a sunny winter day. I had gone up and down the tower, and felt pleased with myself for having taken this initiative, when, outside the little door at the foot, a blind man came toward me. He was a pale, thin man, with sparse black hair and dark glasses that gave him an impenetrable look. He kept close to the inner wall of the courtyard, grazing it with his arm. On reaching the door, he touched the jamb and sharply turned inside. In a moment, he disappeared up the staircase. I stood still, looking at the empty space left by the open door, and at the little plaque that said "To the Tower" nailed to the wall. I felt compelled to follow.

I didn't follow closely. I caught up with him in the ticket office. There I was surprised to see the attendant selling him a ticket as though he were any other visitor. The man fumbled for it, sweeping a little space of desk with his hand until he had it, but the attendant didn't seem to take any notice. Then, with the ticket in one hand and touching the wall with the fingers of the other, he reached the staircase leading to the terrace.

I stood by the desk, watching him until he was out of earshot. "That man is blind," I said to the attendant, and expected him to show some concern, but he just looked at me with his sleepy eyes. He was a heavy man who seemed all one piece with his chair and desk. "He's blind," I repeated.

He looked at me vacantly.

"What would a blind man want to climb up the tower for?" I asked.

He didn't answer.

"Not the view, certainly," I said. "Perhaps he wants to jump."

His mouth opened a little. Should he do something? The weight of things was against him. He didn't stir. "Well, let's hope not," he said, and looked down at a crossword puzzle he had begun.

The blind man was now out of sight. I turned toward the staircase.

"The ticket," the attendant said, rising from his chair. It seemed the only thing that could move him.

I handed him a fifty-lira piece, and he detached a ticket from his book. Then I hurried up the staircase.

The man hadn't gone as far as I imagined. Much less time had passed than I thought. A third of the way up the tower, I heard his step. I slowed down and followed him at a little distance. He went up slowly, and stopped from time to time. When he got to the terrace, I was a dozen steps behind. But as I reached it, he wasn't to be seen. I dashed to the first corner of the bell tower, around the next, and saw him.

He was facing the cathedral, and had I not known that he was blind I would have said he was enjoying the view. Soon he withdrew from the crenel and began walking toward me. He touched the wall, not like one who is groping in the dark but as the blind do. Their fingers touch objects lightly. If they use a cane, this seems alive, a part of them, as sensitive and sharp as a cat's whisker. I moved out of his way, and he passed by me. When I had seen him below, he had seemed eager, taut, and in a hurry. Now he looked as though he had found what he wanted. His gait was calm, and his face had lost its tautness. He ambled over to the other side of the terrace. I didn't feel anxious about him anymore, just mystified. Often he stopped, retraced a few steps, then went on again. Sometimes he seemed to expose himself to the light breeze, sometimes to take shelter behind a merlon. He climbed up to the second terrace. I went, too. We lingered there, he strolling about, I looking at the view.

At last, after ten minutes, I approached him. "Excuse me," I said with the greatest courtesy I could summon, "but I am very curious to know why you came up."

"You'd never guess," he said.

"Not the view, I take it, or the fresh air on this winter day."

"No," he said, and he assumed the amused expression of one who poses a puzzle.

"Tell me," I said.

He smiled. "Perhaps, coming up the stairs, you will have noticed—and yet, not being blind, perhaps you won't—how not just light but sun pours into the tower through the narrow, slitlike windows here and there, so that one can feel the change—the cool staircase suddenly becomes quite warm, even in winter—and how up here behind the merlons there is shade, but as soon as one goes opposite a crenel one finds the sun. In all of Siena there is no place so good as this for feeling the contrast between light and shade. It isn't the first time that I've come up."

He stepped into the shade. "I am in the shade," he said. "There is a merlon there." He moved into the sunlight. "Now I am opposite a crenel," he said. We went down the bell tower. "An arch is there," he said.

"You never miss. And the sun isn't even very strong," I said.

"Strong enough," he said, and added, "Now I'm behind a bell."

Coming back down onto the terrace, he went around it. "Light, shade, light, shade," he said, and seemed as pleased as a child who, in a game of hopscotch, jumps from square to square.

We went down the tower together. "A window there," he said, up near the top. "Another window," he said, when we were halfway down.

I left him, gladdened as one can only be by the sunlight.

The Conversationalist

I WON'T try to reproduce her conversations. I couldn't
do it. Even if I had a tape recording of them, I could not.
They wouldn't come alive again in all their vigor. For how
could one forget the time that has intervened, ignore the
gap, the knowledge that she and others who took part in
them are no more, that the house they took place in is
sold, changed almost beyond recognition? Their im-
mediacy would be lost. For they were not meant to be
recorded, or even remembered. They just happened,
spontaneously, for their own sake only, not to prove anything or to score a point, but as an end in themselves. And
then how could one conjure up the many things they
depended on—the Tuscan breezes that came in through
the open windows, perfumed with flowers and foliage,
like a greater breath to mix with ours? Sometimes a firefly
wandered in as on a visit. And the flavor of the wine; the
warm orange light from the little silk lampshades that
illumined us and cast a thousand shadows from above;
the hand-painted terra-cotta plates; the homemade bread;
the produce of the farm; and, more than anything else, the
company—including the maid, who quite often lingered
by the table to overhear or join in the conversation, and
the smiling cook, who sometimes came in, proud of her

dishes. The house, too, its age, its breadth, its weathered, solid walls.

It was three or four hundred years old, the house. Originally, it might have been a monastery. Later, until the time we bought it, it was in one family for two hundred years. We were there for forty-five. Compared to those who had it for two hundred, we were only sojourners there. But we left our mark, indelible. Perhaps it belonged to us and we to it more than we knew. Perhaps we were more firmly rooted there than anybody else. Whether in my family or in another, life and love were born and died there again and again, yet I cannot help but think that our life was more intensely lived, that our experience made a deeper mark there than other people's. I might be deceiving myself, but I don't think so. It is no empty vaunt. In some ways, I wish that our sojourn had left only a superficial mark, had only scratched the surface, and that we had passed lightheartedly as in a vain, brittle, fickle dance. But frivolous our sojourn had certainly not been. The Second World War was at the center of our stay, astride it, and the dramatis personae themselves were anything but fickle. On that stage, in that house, my mother was the best actress. And, in our forty-five years there, it was during the nineteen-fifties that the conversations around the dinner table reached their peak. My mother was in great spirits then, looked better, more alive than ever. In 1950, to make ends meet, we had started taking in paying guests—most of them friends or friends of friends from America and from England. It was a cheerful venture. Her animation grew with the company, the audience. And taking paying guests certainly improved our difficult financial situation. Until that time, what money we had came from the land we owned, which we kept selling, acre after acre.

We had continued sinking into debt because none of us had much business sense. We were none of us careerists or at all aggressive. In fact, I can remember my mother saying to us once, as if to console herself about the straits we were in, "Well, at least no one can say you are pushy."

My father was a philosopher who didn't teach but simply wrote at home. Oh, he tried his best to make the estate pay for itself—planted thousands of fruit trees, for instance—but it was an unequal task. More than for anything else, he cared for his philosophy. The self-sustaining, the underived, was what he had at heart, what moved him to walk up and down his room, deep in thought, through the long nights. The *causa sui*, an original, active principle, the principle of indeterminacy, the concept of potentiality. In the house, the words had a familiar ring from his constant repetition of them. He wanted to get to the kernel, the node of the problem life posed, the problem of thought and of matter, their relation, their inextricable, intimate kinship or union. And he had to promote his ideas. He thought the questions were vital. His books and articles came out, but his work never obtained the recognition that he hoped for and that perhaps was its due. To expound his philosophy he went on a lecture tour in America and England for a year, then returned home and continued his work, little known, neglected, and even ignored by most philosophers, but unperturbed, undiscouraged.

I had studied medicine, and I did research and practiced for a time, but I was more interested in drawing sketches of people and of places than in the condition of my patients, and it was hardly fair to them. After some years, I quit.

My elder brother was the most single-minded of us. He had taken up Greek and Latin at an early age. At school, he outshone his professor of classics, spent long hours studying, and filled his room with books. He won a scholarship to Oxford, but he, too, wasn't ambitious in a worldly way. He taught here and there, as a replacement, in various high schools in Tuscany and in Umbria. He hadn't the patience, or was too proud, to be a teaching assistant in a university and start the long career of a professor. He preferred to be free, and when he didn't teach, he lived at home, sheltered by his books. Once in a while, he took a trip to see a town, its galleries, its churches, or a girl.

My younger brother had got a scholarship to Cambridge, and, following my father's advice, had begun to study physics there. But he, again, had more an artistic than a scientific bent, and soon, exhausted from undernourishment and overwork, he changed to literature and history. In Rome, he studied architecture for a short time, then gave it up for acting. A Russian director gave him a tryout. The director shook his head but, patting him heavily on the shoulder, said, "Never mind. You, too, are a Karamazov!" After that, he was at home for a while; then he got a job in the Olivetti factory in Ivrea, in Piedmont. Soon he left that, too, and struck out on his own in Milan, importing British goods, and writing poetry now and then.

My sister, the youngest in the family, was rather gypsylike. Gypsies had an inimitable way of dressing, but she came close to it. Sometimes she would doff her gypsy clothes and don a golden Persian dress or an elegant Italian one. She was quite beautiful—tall and sinuous—and could look most striking. Like gypsies, she often went barefoot, and she loved to lounge about the house in the most restful poses. Whenever gypsies came to the house, she insisted on giving them all sorts of food, and once— to the consternation of the cook and maid—she asked them to spend the night there. She also liked to tell people's fortunes, reading their palms, or cards, or tea leaves. And she travelled a lot—even out of Italy, as far away as the Gold Coast—on very little money. She had a gift for portrait painting, and had a show in Rome. Then, all of a sudden, she stopped painting the human form and painted, instead, patches of color with sharp, straight contours. To guide her through them, there was no mark or point save in her mind. Most of her paintings were huge, and she worked them and reworked them, sometimes taking more than a year over one canvas. She had a rather exalted view of them, and when they didn't get the praise she thought they deserved she lavished it on them herself. She made little effort to sell them, sold them only rarely, but she didn't seem to care.

My mother painted, too, but never had an exhibition. Her paintings—landscapes and flowers—were hung here and there about the house, or kept in cupboards. A few she gave to friends. She didn't often paint, but when a bright, happy moment came she was moved to. Then quickly, almost slyly—so no one should stop her—she would get out her colors and her brushes, a canvas and a chair, and go off into the fields. To pay the bills, with a typewriter in front of her and the Shorter Oxford English Dictionary at her side, she typed for long hours of the day and night, translating Thomas Wolfe for Mondadori. But she only got a thousand lire—less than two dollars—a page, and the bills the estate received were crushing. She worked steadily on. For a year, she even took a job teaching art in a village school twenty miles away, and every morning she set off walking to the railroad station.

Then, in 1950, someone had the idea of taking the paying guests. The house had a dozen bedrooms, and across the courtyard and the chicken yard there were two other buildings with more rooms. The paying guests were young Fulbright Scholars from Rome, as well as artists, musicians, writers, critics. Old friendships were renewed and new ones made. With usual guests in the past—and there had been many—the vexing question often came up: How much longer are they going to stay? But not with paying guests. They didn't mind paying the modest prices. They had breakfast in the garden here and there, and lunch and dinner round the huge oval table with the family. Many of the guests were amusing. Some were brilliant. There was plenty of wine—an endless supply of it in the cellar—and wonderful fruit from my father's orchard. The cook, who had grown up in the Chianti hills, worked with extraordinary skill in the kitchen, and sent in the tastiest dishes. Everyone loved her, and they loved the maid, small and smart, as well as other women from the neighborhood who came to help. The meals seemed not so much meals as dinner parties. Now that my mother had money, she could buy linens, pottery, and all kinds of badly needed things. With the maid and the cook, she would sometimes happily go shopping in Siena or, better still, in Florence. She liked especially buying dishes at the market in Montelupo—hand-painted dishes, with flowers, fruit, vegetables, leaves, sometimes a bird or a landscape, done always with a flair, the brushstrokes free, the colors fresh. She loved, too, baskets—the strong, thickly woven ones—and homespun sheets and towels. She embroidered napkin holders with various flowers, sitting out in the garden where these flowers grew, and using the needle and thread as if the needle were a brush, the thread the pigment. She filled the house with a warm radiancy, and could impart her enthusiasms and gladness. Many of the paying guests, particularly some of the younger ones, really loved her.

But the best thing of all, almost everyone agreed, was to hear my mother speak or tell a little story—as about an elderly woman who helped in the kitchen and who had a daughter, a girl of about twenty, who had been working in town as a maid for a family. Once, my mother heard the woman telephoning the family to say that her girl wasn't going to be working for them anymore. Though the lady wanted to know why, she gave no reasons and made up no excuses, but simply said quite cheerfully, "My daughter isn't coming anymore . . . she just won't be coming any longer . . . she isn't going to come. . . ." And no matter how much the lady pressed her for a reason, she just stuck to those few words. Or when my mother told of a woman called Giuseppina, who once said to her, "Oh, I was supposed to've had a beautiful name—Solange—if my mother had had her will. But when my father got to the town hall, which was a long way from home, he forgot it. So the clerk said, 'Yesterday was San Giuseppe. Why don't you call her Giuseppina?' " Little things like that, but my mother could make them zesty. They had the unadulterated flavor of the countryside around the house. From her one got it whole, authentic. And she knew the farmers' special, rare words for the wheat's first greening and for its later stages, their adjectives for wine, the words with which they described the underground struggle of the seed. Sometimes my mother would get very excited, especially when talking about political intrigues and scandals—as when she told of Pius XII, deathly ill, at the mercy of a quack doctor he trusted, and the hubbub at the Vatican about it. To some such sad thing, the way she told it, the guests would listen with glee, for she conjured up most vividly the world of whispering nuns and cardinals and priests, as well as the angry doctors who had been excluded.

She liked to sit on at the table long after the meal was over, with a crust of bread and a glass of wine. Often my sister would try to get the guests to move to a sofa and more comfortable chairs in the next room, which was separated from the dining room by an open arch, but she couldn't take them away from my mother. My sister would get up and go to lie down on the sofa, and, seeing that no one followed her, she would sometimes return and again suggest that they come over. But still she couldn't budge them. They would hardly even notice her. I would look at the absorbed expression on their faces, and at my mother speaking—unself-conscious, un-rhetorical, striving for no effect, heart and soul in what she said, her identity completely taken up by the persons, the places, the situation she was telling us about, her eyes keen, and the lines of her face admirably serving to convey all her impressions. And the guests sitting there listening to her seemed a tribute to the power of conversation: the chairs around the table weren't very comfortable, the sofa and the armchairs *were,* my sister *was* attractive, but—young men though some of them were—there they sat, oblivious of all that.

The Orchard

"THEY all have this prejudice against fruit trees," he keeps saying.

Though no one wishes to remind him, there is some reason for it. Thirty-five years ago, when he was forty-three and a novice to agriculture—philosophy until that time had been his only field—soon after moving to the Tuscan estate his father bought him, with extraordinary energy he set himself to looking for spring water, of which the house was till then deprived, found it ("It was there," he said), ordered two hundred peach trees from a nursery in Pistoia, and had them planted down on a fertile plain below the spring. Peaches, he claimed, would fetch far more than wine, wheat, or olive oil—the produce that the farmers in this, the Chianti, region prized. In the nearby town, he argued, much of the fruit had to be brought in from far away, so that there surely was a market here for perishable fruit like peaches, plums, apricots, and cherries—but especially for peaches. Peach trees grew fast. "In three years, they begin to bear," he said, and started counting, though when not on the subject of fruit trees he was fond of quoting the Latin dictum that he who begins to count begins to err. The figures he came to! Two hundred trees by twenty kilos by two lire. Eight thousand lire from just two hundred trees. Walking the fields, looking at the ground, hands clasped behind his back, he had his sons excited. Only the farmers remained skeptical. They understood vines, olive trees, and wheat. Anything else they rather distrusted. Their attitude didn't daunt him. It only made him bolder.

In the moist soil of the plain, the trees grew well, and in the fall he ordered more—three hundred this time. "Five hundred trees by twenty kilos by two lire," he now said. In the spring of their second year, the little trees had their first blossoms—the most delicate pink, a few to each plant. One or two became peaches—tiny slips of substance with a silvery, soft fuzz ending in a cowlick. At first the faintest green, they swelled, they reddened, they were ripe. And at the same time the price of wine was falling. It cost less than a lira a bottle—hardly a dime. He joked about it. "Please, *please* have another glass and help us drink it." Wheat, too, was low, and so was olive oil. Only the taxes rose.

But in the plain the five hundred trees, growing up and florid, promised harvests that would once and for all solve what he called the "disastrous financial situation." In the house, one heard a lot about it. "The water is level with our throats," he'd say, creating a feeling that made everyone uneasy and drew long sighs from his wife. "But oh, dear me, what can we do?" she'd say, stretching her arms down in a helpless gesture. Any big new purchase was put off till the peach trees would start producing. And in the meantime, to save on electricity, he bought weak light bulbs. The house grew dim. Never mind, his eyes were on the trees.

Every day, over his shoulders the threadbare charcoal-gray mantle he had worn since his young days when he had climbed Mont Blanc, the Matterhorn, the Giant's Tooth, Monte Rosa, and a hundred lesser peaks both of the Alps and of the Apennines, he would go down to the plain to look at his peach trees.

The next March, there weren't just one or two blossoms to each tree but myriads. Each flower a peach. Well, perhaps not quite. Say three to one—three blossoms to one peach. Say even four to one. He counted the blossoms on a branch, and then the branches; he divided by four to be on the safe side; again he divided, to get the weight in kilos; then he started multiplying. It was like coasting on a bicycle down a mountain road and having the horizon at one's feet. He looked at the plain, only a portion of which had trees. "If all goes well," he said, "we'll plant some more."

All *did* go well. When the wind blew away the petals of the blossoms, there remained the greenish-white, tiny, rounded mass. A little bead of fluff it seemed at first, but if you squeezed it you felt it was pulpy even then, and if you squashed it there was a green smear left on your thumb. That downy light green was alive, and it clung hard by its minuscule stem. It was not about to drop or to come off at the least touch. And it seemed as though there was no blossom that did not turn into a fruit. The peaches were so thick that here and there the trees had to be thinned. When the peaches ripened, he hired some help—mainly girls from nearby farms—to pick them. Into the barn came the full baskets and the crates, filling it with fragrance.

"They are as beautiful as flowers," he said, watching the fruit being put in rows and layers inside the boxes.

From town, the buyers came with their wallets bulging, and the trucks left with heavy loads. There were so many peaches they tempted thieves. After some had been stolen, a barbed-wire fence was set up around the orchard, and a big white shepherd dog put there to guard it. Signs claiming the peaches were from his farm appeared on the pushcarts in the squares. He beamed. He saw the world peach-colored. So he ordered more trees—a thousand this time—and since the water of the spring wasn't sufficient to irrigate them all, some workmen who specialized in building wells dug a trench, spectacularly deep and long. Enough water was found to irrigate three or four thousand trees. To him agriculture was irrigation and fruit trees. Even as a child he had had a passion for water and watercourses. Once, he ran away from home and was found with a bundle on his back, walking along a stream, trying to trace it to its source. And now nothing was nicer than in a summer drought seeing water gushing out and making mud of the dry, the brittle earth—nothing more beautiful than fruit or than girls picking the fruit.

The blooming that took place the following spring! The bees seemed driven crazy. They buzzed from one blossom to the other, gathering pollen, bringing it around. Again the blossoms blew away petal after petal, leaving the tiny, almond-shaped, thin, fuzzy peaches that by and by swelled and captured color from the sun, except where the leaves cast their sharp, sleek shadows on them, and, swelling more and more, became so heavy some of the branches had to be sustained. Again the girls came, and the buyers. Again the trucks left laden. Again the farm's name appeared on the pushcarts. And before winter two thousand more peach trees were planted.

That made thirty-five hundred on the plain, and there were other fruit trees near the house—apricot, cherry, plum, persimmon, apple, fig, and pear. The peach trees were of several varieties, from the early kind, which ripened in June, to some that got ripe in November. Foreign-sounding names like Hale, Crawford, and Late Elberta became household words. In the next season, he said, there would be at least fifteen hundred trees producing.

Winter came. Now the peach trees stood, bare of their foliage, in long, stern rows down in the plain, asleep and silent except when the wind blew strong, and then it whistled through them and they seemed to stir. They stood naked, yet so far from dead: each tiny twig intact, waiting and ready—heedful almost. Then in March a softening of the air, and very quickly, as if they could wait no longer, the first buds, the blossoms, and their petals falling to disclose the velvet of the newborn peach. Still March. Mist and gentle showers, and the sun shining out of speckled clouds; then clouds fringed with silver, followed by skies completely overcast. For days there was no sun, no stars, but under the dim days and the black nights the peach trees were safe, as though under a cover. Then, late one evening, the two flag-shaped, rusty weathervanes over the house were heard distinctly turning on the roof —a grating, creaking sound. Slowly they turned, taking what seemed a long time about it, opposing as they did a fair amount of resistance to the wind and indicating a marked change in its direction. It was the north wind. Quickly it cleared the sky. Over the house now, the stars were shining in all their wintry brightness. One couldn't help but admire them. But to the not so different blossoms on the plain this change of wind, this polished starlit sky was baneful, and all the members of the household knew it. In the morning, when they woke up, the sun was shining, the fields down in the valleys were hoary and stiff with frost. A workman who had got up at dawn reported that in the plain the frost had "burned" all of the peaches.

"All of them?"

"Hardly any left, you'll see. Why, it was like crunching through snow down there this morning," he said, and swore, impressed—no, almost awed by what nature could work when it put its mind to it. A robust frost, no doubt.

[19]

In the next few days, its full effect became apparent. The tiny, beadlike peaches, as you could readily see if you cut into them with your thumbnail, were black inside, had lost their firmness, had a shrivelled feel, and they came off at the slightest touch, without a sound, as if they were bits of matter that had got there by chance. On tree after tree, one looked in vain for a whole peach, for one that wasn't black and wizened.

The leaves came out of the buds, deep green and thick, so thick sometimes that you parted them to see if by chance they weren't hiding a peach. But you would never find one.

"Still, the trees are growing," he said, unperturbed. "Without fruit they may develop more, and next spring we'll try and protect them."

In the late fall, he bought an extraordinary number of cane mats, put up tall poles along the rows of peach trees, strung wires from pole to pole, and in March, just before blossomtime, hoisted the mats up. At the same time, he had piles of kindling, brambles, and moist straw placed here and there ready to be burned if a cold night should come. A cold night came—frosty, sparkling with stars. The fires were lit. The smoke rose, hiding the stars. And the mats hung like magic carpets over the three thousand five hundred trees. But in the morning, when the sun rose in the blue sky, the little peaches had fared no better than the previous year.

Another summer without fruit. Though fruitless, the trees still had to be pruned, the ground around them hoed and irrigated. It was discouraging, however; the workmen clipped and dug without believing in their work.

The following March, the mats went up again. They could be seen from the main road—a tented army. Some passersby wondered what they were. And those who knew laughed or made remarks like "The good money he wasted on that place!"

"Two good seasons and two bad ones," he said. "We have an even chance."

In March, there was no frost. No frost in April. The peaches, tens of thousands of them, were fair-sized. "They are out of danger now," everyone confidently said. Then, on May 2nd, the frost. The spectacle this time was worse than it had ever been. The peaches withered, and grew as black as mushrooms rotting, then fell from their branches. The workmen shook their heads. "That plain is lethal," his wife said, but he—he took it in his stride, like the philosopher he was, and continued hoping.

It was clear, though, that those first two good years had been exceptional, for the following spring, too, there came a deadly frost. The land—valuable, fertile land—could not be kept unproductive. The older peach trees were cut down; the younger ones were left in the hope that there might be a crop. There wasn't. Not for two more years was there a good season. By then, however, the Second World War had broken out, and he, being Jewish and alert to what might happen, had taken the family out of Italy to England, leaving the estate in the care of a bailiff. For the duration of the war, the peach trees were forgotten. For so long they had been the subject of so much conversation, and now suddenly they didn't matter anymore.

After the war, in 1946, when the family returned, of the three thousand five hundred peach trees only two trees were left. They stood by the barn, old and barren, many of their branches without leaves. Why they had been spared nobody knew. Perhaps because they weren't in anybody's way, perhaps to stretch a clothesline to—there was a font nearby where women did the washing. Or perhaps just as a souvenir.

But if the trees were gone, his passion for them wasn't. He read an American pamphlet on peach trees, which one of his sons had sent for and given to him. It was one of those booklets that the American government prints and sends out free upon request as a public service—a plainly written, informative thing. The choice of location for an orchard, it said, was crucial; since warm air tends to rise and cold air fall, in hilly country where there's danger of frost peach trees ought never to be planted at the foot of hills or on a plain, no matter how fertile and rich in water that low ground might be. Scarcity of water, it stressed, was far less dangerous than frost, since very little could be done to save the peaches on a frosty night, while in a drought the trees could be irrigated wherever they might be. These remarks were so pertinent that they seemed a comment on what had happened, and read as though they had been written for him. "Not one of those agricultural experts I consulted ever told me," he said.

He began again, went right ahead and planted a batch of peach trees high on the slope of a hill above the plain. People cautioned him. Irritated, he said, "Everyone is against fruit trees," and he complained about this "hostile attitude" as though it were absurd. If someone mentioned the word "frost" to him, he patiently explained that since warm air rises and cold air falls, up on the hill where the new orchard was, frost wasn't a danger anymore. And he repeated his old arguments in favor of peach trees—about the good market for perishable fruit in the hill town, about the low price of wine and wheat. People looked at him. They knew better than to contradict him. They knew that if they did he would come looking for them wherever they were—in their bedrooms, even—and bring up the subject almost as though they were heathens who had to be converted. One knew his step approaching, knew what was on his mind, knew what he would say, and either one didn't answer or was reduced to saying, "Oh, well, maybe you are right."

He certainly planted the trees with conviction; they were a sort of cause. It was as if some future need, hardly surmised or suspected, were directing the course of his actions. And there was no dissuading him. He went straight on putting all his savings into the new orchard, selling his shares, keeping workmen on it. They brought water to the new plants in a barrel on an oxcart. And he himself, though frail and aging, was often seen going up to the orchard in the heat, his arms stretched by two full pails. Finally, as the trees grew in size and number, he piped the water up to them. To increase its volume, he even repaired an ancient, leaking cistern into which rainwater drained from the roofs of the house.

"Sink money into that hole!" one of his sons said, without considering that his father led a very frugal life indeed and that the money he spent on the orchard was his only outlay of any size.

"What about men who have mistresses, go to Paris, bet on horses, drive expensive cars, drink the best cognacs, or, hypochondriacs, fill the house with drugs?" another of his sons retorted.

"There are those, too."

"He—he smokes Alfas, goes into town by bus, buys a book or takes in a movie once in a while. Why shouldn't he spend money on fruit trees if he wants to?"

"It's all right to say that. But when you see those deep new trenches he has dug—more than three feet deep, you know—"

"After all, the land is his, isn't it?"

Was it his land? Just before the war, in 1938, when the Fascists threatened to confiscate Jewish property, he transferred it to his sons, who, because his wife wasn't Jewish, were exempt from expropriation. In name, at least, the land was theirs. Morally, though, it was still his, for the transfer had been no more than a temporary expedient made necessary by an evil government for an evil reason. Those circumstances were now conveniently forgotten, and when a piece of land was up for sale, as his signature was not required, no one asked for his approval. He became more and more removed from the running of the estate. He cared only for his orchard and his books, went from one to the other, over his shoulders still wearing the cape, as threadbare as an ancient flag, darned many times over.

And now the peach trees on the hill were in their third year, the year in which they were supposed to start producing. He waited confidently. No cane mats or piles of straw and kindling up here. No need. The warm air rises from the plain, the cold air sinks. The stars can shine unutterably bright, the north wind blow, the frost fall. It won't affect them. Not up here, unless, of course, it is one of those exceptionally cold years that come once, and maybe not even once, in a decade, and we all hope it won't be one of those.

A frost came that made the plain and all the low ground white. But the hilltops were green, and so was the slope on which the peach trees stood, all clothed in pink. The cold persisted; sometimes the fringe of white—the frost coating with a silver edge the blades of grass—rose almost to the level of the orchard, skirting it like a tide. Each day, a workman, now become a real expert in fruit trees, disclosed the tiny peaches in their blossoms, and assayed them. They were still whole, still firm, still whitish-green and pulpy, their skin still fuzzy. "So far it hasn't touched them," he reported.

"If they'd been down in the plain . . ."

"Down there, there wouldn't have been one left; you can be sure of that."

The peaches ripened. The girls came to pick them. Girls picking fruit—the way he watched them, the way he spoke about them, sometimes it seemed he wanted nothing more in return for all his labors. Oh, the peaches weren't as large as they had been down in the fertile plain, but perhaps they had more taste. Nor were there truckfuls of them, but every day a station wagon left, loaded.

Each summer, there's a crop. Though he has high hopes and keeps planting peaches, cherries, figs, the orchard hasn't solved the estate's heavy financial situation—but it has solved *his*. At a time when, to pay the taxes, the land has to be sold bit after bit and two of his sons have left to go and live elsewhere—one in Milan, the other in America—he, without having to ask anything from anybody, earns from his orchard enough money for his books, the bus fare into town, the cup of coffee, the movie, the Alfas that he smokes, the little gifts he buys once in a while, and new fruit trees. The orchard fills his needs. Year after year, he watches the trees blossom in the spring, the girls gathering the peaches in the summer.

Of Love and Friendship

MY father was a philosopher, who, right to the end of his life, thought he would make a living from his books. My grandfather, a law professor in Rome, soon saw this wasn't likely to happen and, in the hope that his son could become self-supporting, bought him a country estate in Tuscany, a few miles outside of Siena.

The place was rather remote, and Siena, though a pretty town, wasn't the lively center it once had been. It was, in fact, dormant. Tourism, which before the First World War had livened the town up and which was to liven it up again after the Second, was—with Fascism and the Depression—down in the thirties. The university, though one of the world's oldest, had only the faculties of medicine and law. The hospital, also ancient, was the single busy place except for the market on market days. The schools, most of them converted from monasteries and convents, retained their original bare, ascetic look. On winter evenings the town was positively grim. Stark, too, with its narrow, windy streets. As if the cold and frozen Middle Ages weren't enough, the walls were pasted with death notices, and you were quite likely to meet men in black hoods—members of the medieval confraternity of the Misericordia—leading a funeral procession. The morbidity rate in Siena was among the highest in the nation. Owners of the nearby villas—stodgy, titled people—for the most part passed their time in a club, playing bridge or billiards. My mother would have preferred Florence. Much. But she wasn't used to having her own way, and raised no objections to the choice of Siena.

To make up for its lacks, she and my father—both of whom had grown up in Rome and liked company—invited friends, old and new, to come and stay. There was an eccentric English painter of moonlight scenes. Once, she arrived from Rome sometime during the night, set up her easel in the middle of the drive, and at dawn, her painting finished, rang our doorbell. There was a lanky, clever, spectacled French poet and illustrator in plus fours with the energy of an electric eel. And there was a young woman writer from Florence with long bleached-blond hair and plenty of makeup, a hypochondriac, insanely in love, often in tears. She was supersensitive, had mediumistic powers, and sometimes in her bedroom late at night she, my parents, and another friend would have séances, from which my two brothers, my little sister, and I were always excluded.

My mother was apt to change her mind about company and claim she wanted to be alone. The guests, she said, were fine—very dear, congenial, and all that—but everyone had the right to a bit of solitude. "Soon they'll go and we'll be alone, *cocchino*," she would tell me, and pat my knee. But when they finally did go—and sometimes they stayed for months—she would often fall into a silent, sombre mood. And we looked forward to a visitor, for then—at least at the front door—she would be forced to smile. We depended on her smile. Guests brought it on, and a hundred other things, of course—a brood of newborn chicks, fluffy and golden in a basket, looking up at her in unison, or the sun shining on a newborn leaf, or perhaps a letter. Not my father's jokes, I'm afraid, or his attentions. But a newborn leaf! An urge to draw it, or paint it, or embroider it (she said threads came in a greater variety of colors than did pigments) would assail her, and for a happy day it was a love affair between her and the leaf. She was a painter born. She never had an exhibition, though. She didn't care. She was too modest and at the same time too proud. Beyond worldly contest. A woman busy with the children and the house, and with her husband, who kept calling her—to read a paragraph he had written, to accompany him somewhere, to ask her for advice. She was never too busy to listen, never resentful of being interrupted, always ready to put away her work, though with a sigh. Most of her canvases were hidden in closets when they should have been hung not just in the house but in a gallery, a museum.

The relationship between her and my father: the hardest to imagine, the hardest to describe. Affectionate, loving even, but not passionate, not voluptuous—at least not on her part. Guests sometimes told me what a wonderful marriage my parents' was, that they'd never seen one that fared so well. Oh, they had the highest praise for it, and all the time I knew they were way off. She admired him for his being uninterested in a career, for his taste, for his liberal political opinions, for his tremendous dedication to his work. She believed in his philosophy. He was an extreme idealist, and most of the time she saw him as unassailably right. But she strained to understand his concepts. She was ready to agree with them, but they usually were beyond her grasp, just beyond her grasp; or, if she understood them, she wasn't able to argue with him about them, discuss them with him—only question them, ask questions, which he would answer affably but never in her language. An elusive element ran through his words, which in vain she tried to seize. She admired him, surely, but his thinking was beyond her. He encouraged her; he told her she had a very philosophical mind indeed, for there was no understanding a concept fully—everything needed to be deepened. She said he told her he'd married her because she didn't go by conventional values. Now, she asked, what kind of a reason was that for marrying you?

Did she love him? Or, rather, how did she love him? Almost like a son, like someone who had to be helped, comforted, humored, and consoled. But not quite like a son, either. He was more exacting than a son—irritable, willful, and so determined. At times, if she didn't take notice of something he was saying or misinterpreted something he had said or interrupted him, he would turn against her in a rage. I remember his sharp, hateful, self-righteous tone of voice—no swearing, insults, threats, or even shouts; just the tone. His lips taut. The words that seemed to be uttered by clenched teeth—by nothing soft, like lips or tongue, but only by the teeth. Words that came out rattling like small shot, propelled against her. I remember the silence with which she bore his anger. And rarely, perhaps stretching her arms down and back disconsolately, her replies, in a small voice: "Oh, but listen. . . . What can I say? I'm sorry." She didn't like people to make scenes, and for this reason, I think, she never left the room. I remember the stony silence that would follow, and her gloom.

Sometimes she couldn't stand it anymore. She seemed exhausted, at her wits' end. She wanted to be far away, alone. Once, wistfully, she told me that in her young days a workman had paid her some attention. "He talked to me as I walked along the Tiber. A bricklayer. I wonder what life would have been like with him. Simpler, perhaps. But then I wouldn't have had my little boys, my *ragazzini*," she said, and brushed her palm down my face lightly. And sometimes she would say, "I'll pack a small bag and leave; I feel like leaving; I'm going to leave; oh, yes, I am leaving." But she always stayed. She and he slept in separate rooms, as far apart as the big house would allow. But often he would be calling her, calling her, calling her. . . .

And then about 1936, to save the situation, there came a guest who, especially in my mother's view, wasn't like any other guest we'd had—a complete original, and one for whose departure she never hoped. He would stay with us for a week or two, and come perhaps three or four times a year. No, he wasn't like anybody we had ever seen. Millo, that's what my mother called him. In Siena, he didn't go to the museums or the cathedral but, with a big old leather briefcase and a penknife, he went to the public park. His business was with the trees. He would be seen chipping away at the bark as if he had really come on something. A policeman or other public-spirited citizen would amble over to see just what he was up to. Everyone was curious about him. "Are you after mushrooms? Snails?" Smiling, and in a Genoese accent that sounded strange and worldly-wise to Tuscan ears, he would explain that he was collecting lichens, that this little thing he was cutting off the bark was, in fact, a lichen, and tell them its Latin name. Immediately they would start calling him *"Professore."* If they failed to be impressed, he would go on to say that some lichens had medicinal properties; this was almost certain to rouse their appreciation. Lichens, he told them, weren't parasites. The way he talked about them, they seemed to be possessed of all qualities. The little cut he made on the bark was insignificant, almost invisible, and he would be allowed to continue his pursuit. He had a scalpel and a hammer, too, and sometimes he chipped at a rock—for lichens, like moss, and perhaps more than moss, grew on practically anything and in just about any part of the world, even in the polar regions and the desert. This extraordinary interest, he explained, took him not just to parks and gardens but to deep woods and remote mountains. Ah, he was a cunning one for sure, or mad, and in either case they let him chip away.

Why such a passion? Well, for their beauty, mainly. Pale green and yellow, orange and gray, tenuous blue, silver, and almost white, spread by the wind or growing by contiguity, they improved the looks of almost anything they stuck to. Nor did they interfere with the host, except to give it cover. They made the tile roofs golden. They grew on ugly walls and monuments until their ugliness quite faded. They contributed to the ruins part of their weathered look. They were the hand of time, its patina, its gift, or an instrument it wielded. And if you looked at them closely you saw the marvel of their structure: lacework, filigree, touch-me-not golden curls. Always an adornment on the bare. How did nature manage to be so unerringly tasteful? Was it, as with the clouds, the magic hand of chance?

Soon Millo had most of us enthusiastic about lichens. My younger brother even started a collection of them. My parents bought him a small microscope. With it, one could get lost in the leafy and branchlike maze. Another world, it seemed. Not flat, as in a slide, but three-dimensional, with shadows of its own, a place where hanging gardens mixed with orange goblets and gossamer strands. Millo himself had discovered several new species of lichens. Some bore his name. He had sold collections to Harvard, Columbia, and a number of other universities. We were most impressed.

"I've given them the discards," he would say. He was

only joking; according to my mother, he sent excellent specimens, beautifully packed. "You should see those boxes," she said after she and my father had driven to Genoa to call on him. His own collection was in a state of flux—he was continuously exchanging samples with lichenologists in Sweden and other countries. In Italy he had the field to himself.

"Is this rare?" my younger brother and I would ask him, running in from the woods to the house, and always he would look at the samples with joy and encouraging exclamations. "Oh, oh, look what they've found!"

My mother seemed rejuvenated. It was as if he had borne into the house a gift that brought new life. My father, too, looked through the microscope and marvelled, going as far as to say—I have it from a letter—that the *Cladonia verticillata* had the pureness and beauty of a Donatello. And the cook, who also looked through the microscope, went into praises of nature that sounded something like those of the chorus in Greek tragedy. We went for drives, and now there was more purpose in our outings. "Oh, we've found some rare ones," he would say, and, putting a hand on my younger brother's shoulder once, he added, "And Sandro found one that may be quite new— a new species altogether. Of this I am sure. I've never seen it before; I just don't know it."

Was he serious?

Millo was friendly with my father, listened to him and read his work, agreed with it and praised it, but no more than my mother could he discuss it at length. And with my elder brother, who was very studious and not as fond of lichens as the rest of us, he read Greek—Homer, Aeschylus, and Sophocles. Giving Greek lessons was something he did in Genoa to supplement his income from the lichens, but, as with them, you had the feeling he would have done it quite apart from the money—for pleasure. The thing is, he was a poet. As a very young man, he had written a book of verse, "Thistledown," which had been well received and was still remembered. Now he was about to bring out a new one, "Atiptoe." Brief poems, crisp as his lichens—indeed, so terse that at times it was hard to understand them at first sight.

He would often invite my parents out to dinner. "We are going to the notary public," he would say to us, trying to look serious but unable to look more than half serious. He was a friend of the whole family—of the cook and the maids, too, and of the curate who came to have dinner with us every Monday. But particularly of my mother.

They went for walks together, or, sitting on the garden brickwork, sipped coffee in the sun. Those, I think, were my mother's halcyon days. There was a joy in her conversation that was absent when she talked with my father. The reason was, in part, the subject matter. With my father, philosophy—perhaps some word he was looking for or some problem connected with the publication of a book—a letter he had received no reply to, his hopes for a huge peach orchard he had planted, the heavy financial situation in running the estate. And with Millo the lustre of a leaf, some comic scene in town that morning, how "inconceivably bad" an article was by a writer whom they knew.

My mother, really, did most of the talking. She had this extraordinary verve, which the wine helped, and which someone who listened as he did brought out. He listened with glee. He appreciated her sense of humor infinitely—as if he could listen forever and never have enough. He had the brightest eyes, and the glasses that he wore intensified not just his vision but his looks, added to him rather than detracted; one missed them if he took them off. He was chubby and not tall—shorter than my mother, who was spare and strong. His rounded face tended to the red, perhaps because of his fondness for wine. My father was slim and pale, with large, thoughtful eyes, and was considered very good-looking. As a boy, he had won a prize as the prettiest child in town. So at first I never thought of our friend as a rival to my father. He didn't seem the sort of person to rouse a passion. And then my mother, though she didn't seem as happy with my father as with Millo, had for my father such a strong attachment, such a deep affection, and respect and admiration. Perhaps these feelings—even put together and taken at their height—didn't amount to love, but at that time I was too young to make the distinction. Anyway, except during their tiffs, which I was quite prepared to disregard, I thought my mother loved my father thoroughly, loved him as much as he did her, though in a different way. My father paid a great many compliments to women and said silly things to them—even, and especially, in my mother's presence—but I don't think he was ever unfaithful to her. He had a puritanical streak, an austere control, and an intellectual nature that kept him above gossip or interest in petty things, and took him into a rather remote world crowded with hypotheses and theories.

Well, though I wasn't drawing any distinction between love and admiration, my brother was. Older than I by two years, he began to view the relationship between my mother and Millo with circumspection. He became morose, silent, and reluctant to read further Greek texts with him. He withdrew even more into his room and books. "They're always together," he said to me in a worried tone.

Poor boy, he loved my mother so much, had spent such a lot of time near her, had grown up amid her kisses and caresses, and now he felt the presence of someone else edging, intruding into his place, someone other than my father. My father's love, maybe because of its very nature, had never disturbed him, in the same way that my mother's affection for me, my younger brother, and my sister had never made him jealous. But this did. Perhaps it was that he felt protective toward my father, saw my father rather than himself as left out. At any rate, he began to resent the guest. Oh, not deeply or rudely—if anything, rather pitifully. My mother understood, of course, and I can see her kissing my brother on the forehead and stroking his curls, saying, "What is it, darling? Don't be sad." It wasn't easy to be sad in the house if she was happy, and, indeed, she could not really be happy if anyone in the house was sad. There was something in her of the nurse, the angel. Except, unlike angels, who are ever in a state of bliss, there was no paradise for her as long as anyone was in hell. And so, though my brother could hardly be described as being in hell, his state of mind disturbed her. "Come on, *cocchetto,* come with us to Florence. You need a change. You are always in your books. Let's go. We'll have fun. You and me, Papa, and Millo."

Millo would stand next to him and smile at him amiably. My brother would be persuaded to take the trip, and they would go to Florence, with my father driving his blue, open Chevrolet. And certainly the trip helped my brother's spirits. He would come back with a rare edition of Sophocles, perhaps, wrapped in tissue paper, and treat it as if he were handling a butterfly and barely let me touch it.

"I remember once they went to Rome together," my brother told me quite recently, by "they" meaning my mother and Millo, of course. *I* don't remember, or remember only vaguely. That *he* remembers shows how concerned he was.

Certainly I remember many trips, but most or all of

them were with my father, in his car. We went to the sea, and Millo stayed with us there. And there were trips to the neighboring hill towns, and to Pisa, Lucca, and Pistoia, where my father bought fruit trees in the nurseries, and sometimes even to Genoa, Millo's home town. He always carried his old leather briefcase with him, for his lichens, and took more pleasure in strolling around the public parks than following us into the museums.

Often he would repair to a bar or coffee shop. These were like havens for him. He was a gourmet. In a restaurant he could become almost fierce with the chef if the cooking disappointed him. His usual mild, sweet countenance could turn an angry red. That was about the only aspect of him my mother had difficulty with. It was rare, though. He knew the best restaurants—especially in Genoa. There he would usually take you to the grottolike establishments near the harbor. The kitchen was near the entrance, so the fumes and steam could escape up through the open door. The cooks, usually women, greeted him by name. They would serve him well. They liked him—a real *intenditore* of their art.

He lived with his sister, who was unmarried. She worked in an office and looked after him. Recently, in an anthology, I've seen a poem of his in which she appears as a little girl. The poem is addressed to his father. "Father," it says, in rough translation, "even if you weren't my father I would have loved you, not only because one winter morning, glad, you gave us news of the first violet growing outside the window by the wall, and because you counted for us the lights of the houses as they went on up the mountain one by one, but also because once, as you were about to spank my little sister, you saw her cringing from you and, immediately stopping, you picked her up and kissed her and held her in your arms as if to

protect her from the wicked fellow you'd been a moment
before that."

My mother was forever writing to Millo, and often there
was a letter from him in the mail. Both had the clearest
writing, though there was nothing slow or childish about
it. She wrote her letters on light, pale-blue stationery that
she bought at Pineider, in Florence—one of the few luxu-
ries she indulged in. She used not a fountain pen but a
little wooden pen and nib that she dipped in a brass
inkwell. Sometimes she would enclose a leaf, or a small
drawing of it, or a sketch—perhaps the profile of one of
us or of a guest—the thin line of her sharp pencil supple-
menting her description in quick, strong, black pen
strokes. Sometimes I would watch her as she wrote, and
in her face there was a reflection of the pleasure it showed
when he was present; as she paused between one phrase
and another, I could see that her eyes weren't on me or
on the room but on whatever she was thinking of, and if
I interrupted her she would say, "Be quiet a little now,
love." One could see she put her best effort into her letters
to him. All her letters were spirited and spontaneous, but
those to him had something more—a certain brilliance.
   After her death in 1963, Millo put together excerpts
from them into a small book and published it. The letters
spanned almost thirty years—from 1936 to 1963. "Reading them," one critic wrote, "it occurred to me that many
of us ought to throw away the pen, which in our hands
is a hoe and in hers a little April branch." They were full
of quick flashes, impressions, vivid touches, thoughts
about people, plants, places, books, her work, her mood,
the war. Some of them were written to him from England,
where we spent seven years as refugees during the war
and where for a while he had even thought of coming to

join us; a few from Africa, where she had gone after my sister had a baby there; most of them from the house in Siena; and one or two from the Rome clinic, a month before her death.

They were quite innocent, these letters, but my father, who in thirty years had never appeared jealous, now in his old age—he was in his late seventies—seemed to view the book with suspicion. Perhaps it was its form that troubled him—not whole letters but excerpts. The excerpts in themselves weren't compromising, but what about the rest? What had been left out? Why hadn't the opening and closing words or lines been included? No, he didn't altogether approve of the publication. He thanked Millo for the inscribed copy he received, but not with the cordiality of old times, and a word or two he used (which I never saw) upset Millo so much that he wrote assuring me that his relations with my mother had never been anything more than a strong friendship—that, in other words, they had not been lovers.

I thought of my mother's life, of how unreasonably and hatefully angry my father would get with her, of her silences, her patience, her impatience, and her gloom, of the many long winters in the lonely house, and I wrote to him that I was sorry to learn that they had not been lovers, that I wished they had been, for in that case my mother's life would have been richer, happier.

A few years later he died without answering that letter of mine. Now I think I know why: It didn't deserve an answer—if ever there was a relationship one didn't have to feel sorry about, it was theirs.

The Diagnostician

"OH, my God!" he heard his wife say in the other room. He was sitting at the dining-room table, with a glass of wine in front of him and a cigarette between his fingers. He didn't stir. He was used to these exclamations from her. They meant almost nothing. A crayon mark on the wall, the sight of an ant under the kitchen sink, the baby's transferring books from the bookcase to the floor were all sufficient reasons for them. No, he wouldn't pay any attention. "Anxiety neurosis," he said to himself, and sat there as if nothing further were required of him, like one of those pre–First World War Viennese professors of medicine who, once they had made the diagnosis, lost all interest in a case and left the treatment for their assistants to prescribe.

He took another sip of wine. He wished he had some bread—a hard crust, preferably the heel. "Isn't there any bread?" he complained. None of the family heard him, and they wouldn't have answered or done anything if they had. Too lazy to get up and go into the kitchen, or perhaps viewing such a move as an interruption, he sat and looked at the wine, sat ponderously, a load for any but the sturdiest chair. Even his arm resting on the table seemed to weigh down on it. His hair was long, though, being no longer now than a great many people's, it had stopped drawing comments. He wore an old navy-blue sweater and workman's corduroys. Blue originally, the blue had become a background color. His clothes after a while began to resemble his palette. He was a painter. Once, years ago, he had been a doctor, a practicing physician. "I had a nice little office right in the center of Rome, near the Piazza di Spagna," he would say if asked about his former work, in a voice that seemed to express regret, though more perhaps for the location than the exercise of the profession.

"Do you miss it?"

"No—only sometimes. I got to be too busy. I couldn't paint, or think anymore, which is what I like to do best. So I gave up one art, one medium, for another. What I miss most is my prescription book. With it in my pocket I felt a certain power. You know, the possibility of prescribing anything, anything. . . . It gives you an advantage over the layman. Now I feel sort of dispossessed."

"You can't practice here?"

"No, no, and I wouldn't really want to."

"Why not?"

From the way it was asked, the question carried an implication that his painting wasn't worth his practice. He would look away, almost offended, and think of his paintings tenderly. They revealed to him things that would have lain forever undisclosed. And what if they didn't make him rich? Questions like that made him hate even the thought of money.

Sometimes the children, overhearing the conversation, would gaze at him, and, perhaps hours later, say, "Daddy, were you a doctor?"

"Yes."

"Was Daddy a doctor, Mama?" they would ask unbelievingly, and laugh at her reply. He looked so different from the doctors they had known—especially from Dr. Penrose, spotless, smiling, and smooth-shaven.

No matter, he had been a doctor all right. He looked at his hands. They knew it, and for confirmation he percussed his chest. His fingers moved with the old ease, and the sounds obtained were perfectly familiar—the tap-tap deft, sure, measured, unmistakably a physician's.

He sipped the wine. Presently, his wife walked into the room. "Judy has a big red blotch on her neck."

"Well, call the doctor."

"Can't you come and take a look at her? You're a doctor."

"No."

"Aren't you dreadful," she said, and walked out of the room.

It was probably true. But he wasn't a doctor. And the blotch most likely wasn't big or red, and could wait. Alarmists everywhere, he thought. If they would just let him finish drinking the wine, smoking the cigarette. A little peace, that's what he thirsted for, and it could only be taken in sips. Stubbornly he stayed on at the table, though it was no use now—the wine, the cigarette were no use.

Or were they? Unexpectedly, as he looked at the veils of smoke, scenes from his medical days presented themselves to him, and in the smoke he saw the past. Indeed, he felt that smoke *was* the past—a vast skyscape folding and unfolding, hiding and disclosing, moving, never still, and showing through sudden breaks in the clouds now this, now that portion of your life as the winds shifted. Sometimes you did the shifting—when you tried to remember and searched and peered—but the past was never as clear as when it unfolded before you of its own volition. Never as clear as when it came to you unsummoned. Obedience wasn't its strong point.

In between those shifting veils of smoke, he saw himself—oh, so clearly—as a second-year medical student, at
the university hospital in Siena, Italy, in 1946. Alessandro, a childhood friend, was sick with a high fever, wast-
ing away with it in one of the wards, which, because the
walls were frescoed, hadn't been painted in five hundred
years. A few weeks before, he had been a jaunty young
man with glossy curls and long-lashed eyes, flirting with
the girls by a tennis court, and now he lay in bed, earth-
colored, gaunt, with sunken cheeks and shiny eyes. Behind him rose the immense wall of the ward, with Biblical
figures looking down, watching over, seeming to care.
And he looked at you with the slightly annoyed look
young men who are confined to bed greet you with—a
look that seems to say, "Me here, imagine!" He had been
in the war, in a submarine; he had been captured and sent
to India. He had had so many narrow escapes, and now
—now that peace had finally come and he was back in his
home town—illness had struck and seemed about to take
him under. It was too ludicrous. He smiled. The smile was
strangely altered by the loss of weight, more like a grin.
Could it really be that he was on his way out? His mother
was afraid. She practically lived at his bedside. Her first
husband—the young man's father—had died long ago,
her second husband during the war, when the Germans
had sunk his ship. This sick boy, whose weight seemed
to diminish before her eyes, was her only child.

And the awful thing was that the doctors didn't know
what he had. What *did* he have? There was the fever,
irregular and spiking, that suggested malaria or sep-
ticemia; there was an ache in the lower right chest that
suggested a pulmonary condition. They made tests, they
X-rayed him, they gave him penicillin, but the tests were
inconclusive, the X-rays no help, the penicillin useless,

and he didn't improve. His cheeks became hollower, his eyes looked larger. A certain fear, too, seemed to discompose them.

The second-year medical student, though internal medicine was a third-year course, had recently bought a large textbook of medicine, and he delved into it and into his friend's history. Most diagnoses, he had read, were made from the patient's history, but in this case the history seemed quite negative. The most unusual and significant thing about it was that Alessandro had been in India.

"Were you ever sick in India?"

Alessandro shook his head, bored by the question that he had been asked again and again.

"Never anything?"

"No."

"Not even an upset stomach?"

"Oh, plenty of those."

He read in the book under dysentery, and came to the section on amebic dysentery. Its chief complication was an amebic abscess of the liver, and it could occur long—even years—after the intestinal symptoms had subsided. Indeed, quite often the abscess wasn't preceded by any intestinal symptoms whatsoever. The more he read, the more convinced he became that this was Alessandro's illness. Everything pointed that way. He was quite certain. Excited, too. For the diagnosis seemed like a wonderful key he had found, a key that would open the way to his friend's recovery. He had to go to the doctors, tell them; he felt compelled to. But he was only a second-year medical student. Never mind. Someone's life was at stake. His friend was near the end—it was obvious. He couldn't last more than a few days longer. And they weren't doing the right things for him at all—just making tests, giving penicillin, insisting with it. He should be given emetine and the abscess aspirated; at this late stage he might even need surgery. It was all so clear—how was it that they didn't understand?

Usually shy, but now absolutely without shyness—a man with a cause—he waited in the hall for the head of internal medicine to complete his rounds, and when he saw the professor in his white robe coming out of the last ward, with a train of assistants, he approached. "Sir, may I talk to you about Alessandro Olmi, that patient in—"

"Yes, yes, I know." The professor cut him short, walking on across the hall, not stopping for a moment, hardly slowing down at all, and yet not unwilling to listen.

"Well, he is a good friend of mine. He was in India, as you know, during the war, in a prisoner-of-war camp, and I think he is suffering from an amebic abscess of the liver."

The professor, tall and self-possessed (had that self-possession got him the job?), smiled condescendingly. "No, no, the case is still under study," he said confidently. "But it's not abdominal; it's clearly a chest condition—pulmonary or pleural."

"Oh, but—"

The professor resented the "but," and the smile faded. "Who are you?" he said.

"I am a second-year student."

The professor dismissed him by turning to his chief assistant. The group had now crossed the hall. The student stopped and watched them, watched their smiles. One of them turned to glance at him curiously.

He pondered. A chest condition—no. Now he could only appeal to the young man's mother. He took her aside in the ward and told her what he thought her son was suffering from.

"You should tell the doctors," she said.

"I did."

Another day went by, fruitlessly, wastefully. The agony of knowing and being unable to persuade. "I am sure that's what it is," he said to the mother again, in her son's presence now, and restated his opinion.

Alessandro listened intently.

The mother said she had spoken to the doctors about it, and added, "Let's hope it isn't an abscess, let's hope it isn't," as if hope could alter the situation.

It was maddening. Yet another morning went by in which nothing was done—or, at least, nothing he thought was in the right direction. In the afternoon, he met the professor of internal medicine in the hall, and didn't hesitate to broach the subject once again. "Sir, I am very worried about my friend, Alessandro Olmi. It seems to me—"

This time the professor didn't smile. "Look, we decide," he broke in. "Enough. Go."

He stood, irate, helpless, discounted, then slowly left the hall, anticipating the worst for his friend. But the next morning there was a consultation. The chief of surgery was present. Alessandro was moved to the surgical ward, and that same morning taken to the operating room. An amebic abscess of the liver was discovered and drained, and emetine given. He quickly recovered.

"Yes, there was that," he said to himself, and drew from the cigarette deeply, like a surgeon after a successful operation. He blew the smoke away and watched the commotion it produced. It seemed a picture of his life—not stormy but cloudy and in commotion, full of clouds drifting, merging, blown asunder.

He mused a moment, and considered how the smoke changed from blue to silver as it rolled. He put the cigarette out. The veils of smoke still hung about, but sparse now, spread thin, and the present, the objects in the room, the furniture reasserted themselves, claiming his attention and displacing the past. He heard his wife's step approaching, rapid, bold, determined, as if she were coming on business and wanted an answer quick; her step was accompanied by the heavy thud of bare feet—their ten-year-old daughter's.

"Here," his wife said, "you look at Judy," and Judy stood beside him, almost at attention, waiting, with an alert, expectant look, blinking her eyes.

Slowly he turned toward the tall and sturdy girl who tried to bare her neck by pulling down the collar of her blouse. "No, let me see it properly," he said, and with the ease both of doctors and of lovers he unbuttoned her blouse and slipped it off her. There was indeed a good-sized, reddish blotch at the base of her neck, in front.

"Judy," he said, "have you been dousing yourself with eau de cologne?"

For a moment the girl didn't reply—only blushed a little. "Yes," she said. "How did you know?"

"Oh, there's oil of bergamot in it, and it can do that to you sometimes. Just don't use it anymore; the spot will go away."

"Really?" she said, quite pleased, and lightly hopped out of the room.

Even in a minor thing like this something had struck him from within, and he had known. It was the same as when in painting you realized exactly how things were, when the result surprised you, when something new and live came out of the inert pigment. It was the same, and it didn't matter if you were a painter or a doctor or what you were, as long as such moments came to you—oh, at least once in a while.

The Jump

THERE he was—a tenebrous man—forty-eight, slumped in an armchair of his living room, brooding late into the night. Things were not going well: his wife hostile, his daughter—only a few years ago a cherishable, chubby little girl—spiteful. His fault, probably. With his daughter how had it started? With her not wanting him to teach her Italian, his native language, and his getting angry about it? Or before that? He remembered that once, returning from a trip to New York to show his paintings, he found his family—his wife, his daughters, then seven and four, and his son, three—sitting around a table on the lawn, a picture of happiness, and that a little later, when he had settled down and felt no longer an outsider, as he had in the first few minutes, his wife told him their daughter had said during his absence, "It's so peaceful when Daddy is away."

They are happier without you, he thought. Then what are you doing here? Go away and make them happy. He had vowed to go, threatened them with his going as though it would be a disaster. Why, it might be a blessing. The picture of them around the table on the lawn was indelible, and so were his daughter's words. His frettings, his scoldings, questionings, apprehensions disrupted their simple life. A disturber of the peace, that's what he was. If one of his paintings didn't please him, his dissatisfaction knew no bounds; it wasn't confined to what lay between the stretchers but attached itself to everyone, to everything—nothing was excluded. But if, as sometimes happened with extraordinary ease, he could turn matter into form, get color out of pigment, his disposition improved immensely.

It was miserable now, and he sat in the living room alone that night. Getting along with people—why was it so hard? He hadn't been able to get along with his father, either, or with his sister. Nor, it occurred to him, had he ever had a full, long-lasting relation with a woman, though he had loved, desperately. One might be a brilliant scientist, a real wizard, he thought, and fail utterly with his wife and children. Mercifully, they were now upstairs asleep. Mercifully, it was quiet all around, but inside he had a sinking feeling. His soul shrank inside his heavy frame until his body felt inanimate. In a vain effort to disappear, he winced, he shrugged. And he wished that long, long ago he had taken a step he hadn't taken—a jump, really.

It was in July, 1940, and he was on the Ettrick, a Polish liner taken over by the English when the Nazis invaded Poland. The ship was loaded with German prisoners of war—most of them airmen—and interned civilians: sailors from Italian freighters caught in British waters, and German, Austrian, and Italian refugees, and other Italians who had been living in England. Perhaps three thousand men altogether. He was sixteen then, and he had been picked up by the police in an English boarding school as an enemy alien, which he was only technically, his family having left Italy because of the Fascists. He still wore his school blazer, with a pair of bluejeans he had bought from an Italian sailor for a few shillings when his own flannel slacks had torn. For a while after leaving England, none of the men knew where they were going. At one point, perhaps because of a submarine lurking nearby, the ship veered. "Oh, look, we are going back to England!" he exclaimed.

"If we go back to England, I kick you," a German refugee said to him.

"I love England—I hope we go back," the boy replied in anger, in spite of his excitement at the prospect of crossing the ocean.

Soon the ship was on her former course. What was her destination? One such ship had gone to Australia; another —though at the time he wasn't aware of it—had been sunk, and the Germans and the Italians on board had fought each other in a mad scramble to be saved. Nearly all had drowned. For a long time, his mother thought he was on that ship. But the Ettrick kept sailing west, and it became apparent that they were going to North America —to Canada, probably.

It was nice on the ship. After the big internment camp where he had spent two weeks, he felt perfectly free. He was on deck most of the time. Diminutive though the space allotted to them was, it seemed quite sufficient. Here he could feast his eyes on the sea's wideness. Even in the cabin, which he shared with a dozen others, he didn't feel cramped. But he knew it would soon be different—another camp awaited him in Canada. It would end, this interlude.

He stayed on deck as long as he could, night and day. One night, halfway across the Atlantic, he saw for the first time the northern lights. An astronomer—another Italian refugee—tried to explain the phenomenon to him. He caught a word or two: electrons, cosmic rays. The lights shimmered, danced in the immense silence of the starry night. The ethereal curtains waved—diaphanous, mystic. Seeming to follow some unearthly rhythm, they quickened, glowed, then almost disappeared, only to reappear more intense—seemed to fade and to reassert themselves in turn. There it was, the aurora borealis. And it was going on and on, nearly half the sky's vault taken up with it. In Italy, in England, you might wait years—a lifetime—and miss it. But here in mid-ocean it blazed spectacularly.

Then, a few days later, the first birds, and, like a mauve cloud, Newfoundland. The ship entered the Gulf of St. Lawrence. Was there a river with a wider mouth? At first, the banks were so wide apart they couldn't be seen—then, indistinctly, a cape, a headland. Like open arms, the banks welcomed you. Far away gleamed a white church spire, and rows of white specks—the houses. The river narrowed, and still it was wider than any he had ever seen. Tall, rugged, rocky cliffs rose on each side, pine-terraced. And in the clear summer day, the water mirroring the blue of the sky, the living green of the pine trees, the ancient gray of the rocks, the absence of buildings anywhere near gave him a gleeful feeling that nothing could mar. Darkness came, and, according to one of the sailors, they were at least a whole day from the city of Quebec—a reckoning that, since they were going at a good clip, testified to the great length of the river.

As for him, he didn't want to get to the end of the journey. He stayed up on deck, sitting on the good wooden floorboards, his eyes on the riverbanks, which now were dark shadows under the night sky. Each moment spent on deck was a moment saved; each moment spent down in the crowded cabin seemed wasted. Let them play cards and crab and tell their pointless stories. A few hours before, while it was still light, he had heard one of the German airmen commenting on his age—he was the youngest there—to an Italian sailor who knew a bit of German. *"Jude?"* the airman said. "No, no," the sailor replied for him as he turned away. A little later, a slick, obtrusive Italian civilian had asked to borrow half a crown, which was almost all the money he had. And he had given the big, shiny silver coin to him. Why had he? And why, Jewish or not, hadn't he replied yes to the airman instead of walking away? He hated himself for taking the easiest course. But now on the deck he was away from them all. It was lucky for him that they preferred to be below—lucky and amazing. Amazing, too, that the guards didn't mind his staying up here. They must have figured that no one could escape, that no one could jump overboard and reach shore. The river was several miles wide in most places; the current was probably strong, the water cold. Yet it was July, and sometimes the ship came pretty close to one of the banks, though in the dark it was hard to tell just how close.

A few weeks before his internment, he had won a long-distance swimming race at his school, crossing the bay of the village to which they had been evacuated from an inland town. God, he might very well be able to swim ashore, let himself drift with the current and at the same time edge toward the bank—the south bank, of course, which he knew wasn't far from the United States border. He could see himself reaching the rocks of the bank, hiding, resting, drying himself and his clothes in the first morning sun—he would make an effort to swim fully dressed, and with his shoes on. Aboard the ship they mightn't even miss him. He remembered in Liverpool a British officer's ticking each man off on a counter as he boarded the boat. If a man were missing, it might be laid to an error in the count. Or he might just be given up for lost. "Jumped overboard. Suicide—it could have happened anywhere. Fish fodder by now, most likely." Or if they looked for him—and he should allow for that eventuality—they would have a hard time finding him, the St. Lawrence was so long, the woods so vast.

These thoughts absorbed him as nothing had done before, for nothing, unless it was love, fascinated him as did thoughts of escape, of freedom. Escaping, you became the very living symbol of freedom—its essence, its flag. Very easily he could imagine that a prisoner might take years filing through the bars of his cell and not get bored, but that filing his fingernails, though it took no more than minutes, might bore him to death. He saw himself rushing through the woods southward, ever southward, till he was deep into Maine, eating blueberries, roots. The forest, like some English and Italian woods he knew, must be full of fruit now; there must be blackberries, raspberries, pine nuts. He exulted at the thought.

The ship continued its upstream course. He could hear the waves falling, the impact of the hull on the water, and the sound of the engines; he could feel their vibration, transmitted to the whole vessel. He rose stealthily. There was no one anywhere near him on deck. He looked at the black water streaked with white foam, illumined dimly here and there by lighted portholes and lamps. Now was the time. No one would see him. No one would miss him. And he would be free. No hideous camp awaiting him, no barbed wire, no Fascists around him, or Nazis, or guards. He himself alone in the waters, the ship becoming smaller all the time—soon, from the cluster of lights that it had been, only a point of light, then nothing. Just he and the stars and the river. The steady strokes. The feel of the rocks as he landed. It was too beautiful to resist. A jump away from prison, which was death, to freedom, which was life. He stepped over the railing and stood outside it, holding on with his hands.

But he didn't jump overboard. He stuck to the ship,

magnetized to it, and tamely, hatefully—hateful toward himself—he stepped back inside the railing. Like an automaton, he left the deck and went to the stuffy world below—the lounge and the cabin—drawn to it, it seemed to him now, thirty years later, by all the subsequent events of his life. Another river—that of his own life—had exerted a greater pull over him than the St. Lawrence, and perhaps it wasn't true that if he had jumped it would have been toward life. Perhaps he would have died. Perhaps the body, with its wisdom, had sensed death in those waters. Suddenly he brought the back of his wrist to his lips and kissed it—his body, his life.

Sitting in the armchair, he wished he had jumped and reached the riverbank and the United States and led a different life: perhaps got a job on an apple farm in New Hampshire by telling people he was an English evacuee—didn't he have his blazer with the school insignia to prove it, and wasn't that as good as a passport?—and then later enrolled in the American Army, and died at Anzio or Salerno. Or lived on in some unimagined way, a different person, a stranger to himself. Or yet jumped overboard and drowned. Drowned. He saw himself in his last moment in the water, viewing not, as is commonly believed, his past but his future, what actually happened: the misery of the camp—the year behind barbed wire—then school and college, and the long row of failures right down to the last one with his daughter, his finally sitting in an armchair in his living room wishing he had jumped overboard.

The Chest

THERE the chest stands, in the living room, colossal, the sturdiest thing in the house, though it's four hundred years old. It comes from Tuscany, where it was made, probably in Florence. With its jutting bevelled top and its corniced drawers, it reminds me of a palace, the Farnese, each drawer a floor, the wrought-iron handles like great window frames, and firmly founded on four squat, almost invisible feet. And it reminds me of the man it belonged to—our bailiff—and the way it came to us from him, and his disgrace.

He was thrust upon us, this bailiff, or foreman: thrust upon my father by my grandfather when he bought the estate. The bailiff was from a town near Florence, Siena's old rival, and the farmers on our land—there were ten farms and a villa to the estate—immediately viewed him with suspicion, and before long took an intense dislike to him. He was bossy, this man, loudmouthed, bad-tempered, stocky, quite the opposite of my father, who was soft-spoken and polite and slender. Perhaps my grandfather chose him thinking that my father was too gentle. With my father, however, he was very obsequious, servile even, agreeing with and enthusiastic about everything he said or proposed. That's all my father needed to be won over—someone to agree with him.

"Pietro has a philosophical mind," my father said of him. My father had the idea that anyone, even a child, could comprehend philosophical concepts. Frequently he would air them to me as we walked across the fields. I nodded, and Pietro must have done the same. I won't exclude the possibility that once in a while Pietro might have come up with some felicitous expression as he wondered about life and the universe, or with an apt comment on the sad state the world was in—it was during the Depression, and Mussolini was in power—but I am quite sure he never read a book. To this my father would have said that even an illiterate person could be philosophical, and if one thinks of the utter nonsense that one heard and read in those days, and in these, I suppose he had a point. But really Pietro wasn't very bright.

He had a terrific penchant for locking things up—the granary, the pantry, the wine cellar, the gates—and when my mother told him not to, he stared at her. She insisted, and still he couldn't quite make himself obey her. It just wasn't in his nature to leave things unlocked. Again and again, we had to call him to unlock doors and cupboards. Finally, my mother got him to hang the keys on a board in a room next to my father's study. They were large keys, some almost a foot long, and each key had a wooden tag attached to it by a string. On both sides of the tag he wrote "Key to the Granary," or whatever, the word "key" so large it took up almost the entire tag. My mother laughed about it and brought this up as an example of his stupidity, but my father saw very little wrong with it. Stupidity to him was something else: the denial of certain truths.

My father also liked Pietro for his accent. He came from a town called San Giovanni Valdarno, and the upper Arno basin was, to my father, the cradle of the Italian language. Pietro wrote slowly, with an unsteady hand, and could do simple arithmetic, having gone up to the fifth grade in school and then taken a little tutoring from a parish priest. These skills he used on his ledgers, which dutifully at the end of each month he would bring to my mother to check. She found errors, but they were as often in our favor as in his.

Though about forty years old, he was unmarried. His only relative was our cook, a huge woman who had come with him to the house. He would have fierce arguments with her, scolding her for such trifles as neglecting to tell him to buy salt when she knew he was going to the store. They would both flush, she with pent-up rage, he with the fire of his damnations. Sometimes he shouted so uncontrollably I wondered why the blood vessels in his temples didn't burst.

He didn't drive a car—bailiffs didn't in the thirties—but he had a motorcycle, which seemed much more in keeping with his blustery ways. My father had a car, a blue Chevrolet convertible, a rarity in Italy, and we had two horses and a calèche. This calèche the bailiff would use to go into town on market day. He would get a workman to polish a horse's hoofs, oil the harness, wash the calèche, and off he'd go for the day. He loved going into town, to hang around the post-office piazza discussing prices and to have lunch with the other bailiffs in a trattoria. Little by little, he began going into town twice a week, and then three and more days a week. "He's always in town," my mother would complain, and my father would patiently explain that it took a long time to transact business, that in government offices they made you wait a good long time, and that it was the bureaucracy's fault, not Pietro's. The maids whispered that he had a woman in town and that he called at houses he shouldn't call at. When he returned, he would go and knock at the door of my father's study, and together they would talk about the estate, Pietro always careful not to contradict him. My father trusted him. Once, he gave him an inscribed copy of a book he had just published, and I think Pietro was genuinely grateful and probably even made a brave attempt to read it, though I doubt he ever got past the first page.

The estate was decidedly not doing well, but my father blamed the heavy taxes and the low prices, not the bailiff. Did we think he was no judge of character? He knew his men. Any criticism of Pietro he took almost as a personal insult, and we kept quiet.

A young woman from Sardinia who lived in town was expecting a child by a son of one of the farmers. He didn't want to marry her. Once in a while, she would appear at their house, quite helpless. His family was in a crisis, fearing her brothers in Sardinia, and went to the bailiff for advice. He persuaded the young man to marry her. "You see, Pietro has an eloquence about him," my father said. "He is a very forceful speaker. This is a rare quality in people."

My father never fired anybody and believed that, up to a point, the more people he had working for him the better. A concerted effort couldn't help but right things, he asserted. And so he hired new workmen for the estate and English tutors for my two brothers and me and my sister—also sometimes tutors in mathematics, Latin, and Greek. It was a time of unprecedented unemployment, and, though building a deficit, he was helping people. Nor was he in any danger of bankruptcy. My grandfather kept him solvent.

In 1938, Hitler visited Mussolini, and the anti-Semitic campaign began. Because my father was Jewish, his books could no longer be published. All sorts of restrictions were placed upon Jews. Quickly he decided we must leave for England. One shouldn't live in a country, he said, where one didn't have equal rights. My grandfather, who was very old, chose not to leave. From Rome he would move to the country house, and with Pietro's help look after the estate.

I remember Pietro on the day we left. Harsh though he could be with the cook and with some of the workmen, he could also be quite tender, and had a real affection for us—especially for my younger brother, who was twelve, slight, and endearing, with curly fair hair and playful ways. He lifted him and, weeping, hugged and kissed him. As for my brother, he was much too excited about the trip to cry.

After the war, when we returned by boat from England, Pietro came to meet us in Naples, his socks stuffed with ten thousand-lira notes for us. He also carried two *fiaschi* of wine and a suitcase full of salami, bread, nuts, and cheese.

He was married now; of this we had got word. The cook had been fired abruptly during the war and replaced by one of the maids. I remember my mother saying she felt sorry—especially about the way it was done. My grandfather had died, peacefully, in the house, which had been occupied by German soldiers. Jewish though my grandfather was, a German Army doctor had treated him in his last days and had gone to his funeral. What money he had left us was reduced by inflation almost a hundredfold.

The bailiff's wife wasn't from the countryside but from a little town some forty miles away. She looked like a town woman, too, and dressed like one, disdaining shawls and aprons and anything old-fashioned. She was buxom and liked tight-fitting skirts and blouses. She wore lipstick and had a permanent wave. She wasn't really pretty—her jaw was too heavy—but she was a good deal younger than Pietro, and at first sight one got the impression he had done rather well for himself. Yet soon one saw she had a greedy look, and her smile wasn't open.

Until we arrived, she had been the woman in charge. Now she was in charge only of the poultry. She was proud, too, and probably thought she deserved better things. The bailiff's apartment had been done over, to her taste. I remember odd little triangles painted on a wall. A new bathroom had been put in. The apartment was comfortable, but maybe not quite comfortable enough, and certainly nothing like the villa, a bedroom of which she and Pietro had slept in during our absence. Since she had never seen us before, she certainly had no reason to look at us with any affection, the way the maids did. She withdrew to her apartment, took care of the poultry, for which she received a salary, and we didn't see very much of her. Once, however, I overheard her say something about Jews which surprised me. I can't remember exactly what it was. Just one of those little remarks with the word "but" in them—"They are Jews but they seem all right," or "But they are not like us; they are Jewish." Something of the sort. It surprised me, because such distinctions were never made by others in the house.

The bailiff, perhaps at her prodding, soon got my father to hire an extra man, a *sotto-fattore*, or sub-bailiff, a nephew of his from Florence, a young man with rather expensive habits. Before long, he had borrowed and smashed the car of a family friend who was staying with us. He was better at arithmetic than the bailiff and helped him with the accounts. With this little entourage, Pietro now seemed very firmly entrenched indeed. My father was aging. My two brothers and I were away most of the time at universities. My sister was at school. Then she fell ill with t.b. The advent of streptomycin saved her, but it was two years, during which my mother devoted all her time to her, before she was well. The bailiff had more and more of a free hand in running the estate.

In Italy, there was great economic and political unrest. The farmers, who got a share of the profits from the land but didn't own it, pressed for and got better contracts from the landowners. Some large estates were expropriated and split up. Ours wasn't large enough for that. Still, capital, or principal, was taxed, and we began running heavily into debt.

At this point, a man by the name of Fernando, a Neapolitan who had served as a soldier in my father's infantry company in the First World War, came to our house. He was very devoted to my father, who, he said, had saved his life: their company had been almost surrounded by the Austrians and my father had found a way out. Over the years, my father had often talked of Fernando's courage and great physical strength, and of his temper. Once, during the war, he had threatened my father at gunpoint. My father had burst out laughing, and he had put the gun away. After the war, Fernando got into a family brawl in Naples, in which—accidentally, according to him—his mother and her lover had been killed. The judge was of a different opinion and condemned him to prison for life.

For thirty years he was in prison, and all during that time he wrote to my father. The letters, on strange prison stationery, with the censor's marks, kept arriving. And my father replied each time, sending him money, and once two canaries, which, like the Birdman of Alcatraz, Fernando bred, till in a few years the prison was filled with the singing of hundreds of canaries. Finally, in 1950, he was released for good conduct. He was thin, with sparse gray hair, few teeth, and so pale he looked as if he hadn't been in the sun for thirty years. But it wasn't that, for though my father welcomed him and gave him work

out in the fields, his color didn't improve. The long
confinement had affected his health too deeply for sun
and fresh air to restore it.

We saw no sign of the great physical strength my father
had spoken of. His spirit, though, seemed whole—anything but weak. Soon he had endeared himself to everybody but the bailiff and his wife and nephew. They
looked on Fernando as on one who was undermining their
positions. And with some reason. Fernando was very sus-
picious of them, and in his Neapolitan accent he began to
whisper to us that we were being cheated. My father
didn't believe him. He still blamed the taxes and the new
contracts, which, though he thought they were justified,
were all to the owner's disadvantage. But Fernando didn't
give up.

The farmers liked him. They were more than tolerant.
He was popular all over the neighborhood. No one treated
him with the prejudice or reservations that one might
have toward an ex-convict. And he soon persuaded them
that he was innocent and had been wrongly accused.
"And anyway, even if he was guilty he paid for what he
did," they said, and invited him to their homes. With
dramatic gestures, his soft low voice, and his accent that
sounded rather comical to Tuscan ears, he entertained
them with a hundred stories of fearful crimes, famous
bandits, and cruel guards, all probably quite true, insider
that he was. His was certainly firsthand material, told him
by the very perpetrators of the foul deeds that had filled
the newspapers for a generation. He was also in demand
for reputedly being able to tell expectant mothers if their
babies would be boys or girls. He gave medical advice,
and advice on the *lotto,* the state-owned numbers game, as
well as on the soccer lottery, on which every week he bet
his savings. But his mission, it seemed, was to make my
father aware that he was being cheated by the bailiff. The

estate, he was sure, was heading toward ruin, and he regarded himself as the man who could save it, thus repaying my father for all he had done for him. Perhaps also, though he had no experience as a farmer, he saw himself as the next bailiff.

My father continued to trust and admire Pietro, however, and if anyone ventured to talk against him my father would come to his defense and ask, as he had before, in a hurt voice, "Do you think I can't judge a man's character?"

"But let me tell you," Fernando would plead.

"Besides," my father would add, "my wife goes over the accounts carefully every month."

"Oh, the accounts!" Fernando would counter, and make a spiralling gesture with his hand.

My father would get angry.

Fernando looked thwarted, but he persisted.

My younger brother was most receptive to his insinuations. My elder brother was a scholar of the classics, and though he listened patiently to Fernando's accusations he didn't do anything about them. At most he referred them to my mother. I was studying medicine at the time, was home only on vacations, and I tended to take my father's side, believing that my mother would have been able to spot any errors, deliberate or not. Not so my younger brother. He had studied mathematics at Cambridge, and he had a sharp mind for anything that had to do with figures. He took Fernando's allegations seriously. Secretly he began investigating, checking the accounts my mother saw against the bills, and, when they weren't detailed enough, checking with the stores and offices in town that we did business with. He checked the supplies in the granary and the cellar, talked with the farmers, went over old records, and weighed and sifted the new information that Fernando constantly brought to him. The more my brother looked, the more he found, and each new find seemed to give him an enormous pleasure, as if he were discovering gold, and not a loss. He was at a period of transition in his life, not knowing what to do with his degree, and this work as comptroller, carried on in secret, helped his spirits, roused him out of a kind of lethargy and depression. The fraudulent losses he discovered climbed from several hundred dollars into the thousands, growing more frequent and larger as the transactions that he examined became more recent. The bailiff, prodded by wife and nephew, had evidently got bolder and bolder as time went on. My brother was amazed. "Another year like this one and they'll be the owners," he said.

At a certain point, they sensed that something was up. They became very silent and reserved, even with my father. Now my brother went into the bailiff's office while he was there and came out with stacks of papers to examine. Again and again, he would go in and come out with more. Finally, one day he confronted the bailiff with all the evidence of fraud he had uncovered. It was overwhelming—enough to send him to jail. Some of the findings, like purchases that hadn't been made, were very glaring, impossible to attribute to careless error. He took it upon himself to fire him and his nephew there and then, and threatened them with a lawsuit.

I remember my father at supper that day. "And you always thought you could judge people's characters so well," I said to him reproachfully. Coming from me, who until then had always supported him when he defended the bailiff, the words stung. Friends, I'd heard my father observe, always said the worst things, because they knew what hurt. He looked at me. All through supper he had appeared resigned to the bailiff's dismissal and had even managed to counter some of my brother's arguments fairly well, but now, his lips twitching and his eyes shining, he rose from the table and made for the door.

The three, afraid of a lawsuit, which wasn't pressed, left quickly, taking their modern furniture from the apartment but leaving the chest, which was perhaps too old for the wife's liking. They never asked for it and it was never sent to them. It stayed—a kind of forfeit for all that they had taken.

For a while, there was new hope in the house as my brother took over the running of the estate. The farmers who worked our land came to him with words of encouragement, but he didn't really want to be a bailiff, not even on his own land; he said he wasn't interested in agriculture. Fernando didn't get the job and soon left for Leghorn, where one of his acquaintances had invited him to join in some business venture. He got married, we heard, and for a while he seemed to be well off; then his partner's business failed and he resumed writing to my father. My brother found a new bailiff, who was very sure of himself and only half listened to my father. The estate didn't prosper under him, either. If we were able to hold on to the house, it was because my mother opened it to paying guests from America and England. Sometimes in the summer we had more than twenty staying there.

Then, in the sixties, my mother died, and some years later my father. Four years ago, my brothers, my sister, and I sold the house and what was left of the estate. The furniture we divided among us. The chest was one of the things I got, and it came across the ocean to my home on Cape Cod, where it still stands. Sometimes I look at it and open the drawers, and see not the linens that my wife has put there but Pietro lifting my young brother in his arms, my father leaving the table, the empty house.

The Bed

THE bed lay unmade, a Civil War officer's folding iron bed that had belonged to his father-in-law. He remembered seeing it—unmade, just as it was here—in the home of his in-laws, at the top of the stairs in the back bedroom. The door was open, and he had looked in. Besides the bed, the room contained a ladderlike staircase that went up to the attic, a few cardboard boxes, a hard chair, a metal desk with some papers scattered over the top. A Spartan sort of bedroom (though his father-in-law was anything but Spartan; poor man, he liked his comfort). Across the hall, facing south, also with the door open, was the master bedroom, where his mother-in-law slept.

The arrangement was similar to the one here in his own house. Here, too, there was a small room at the top of the stairs, and he slept in it, in the army bed. Opposite, in the master bedroom, facing south, slept his wife, with two of the children—one of them beside her in a double bed, the baby in a bassinet. A third child, the eldest, slept in an adjacent room, though sometimes she, too, crowded in with her mother and sister; he would hear a moan, then the tread of her bare feet as she hurried over to her mother's room. The children, first one and then the other, had taken his place, and he had shifted to the army bed, where he slept alone, pining for the comforts of a double one—like his father-in-law and, long before him, the Civil War officer for whom it was made. It had been his for three years now—ever since the house of his wife's parents was put up for sale after her mother's death and her father's subsequent remarriage. Then, gripping with one hand the head- and footrails of the bed (when folded, it came together in the middle), straining under its weight but unable to stop on the way down the narrow, steep staircase, he had carried it outside to his car and on to the apartment they had had in town, and, a year later, to the house they had bought in the country, up that staircase with it, to his present room.

Its being a Civil War bed gave it a certain distinction. Its having been his father-in-law's bothered him, however, for it pointed to the similarity in their situations—they had both been reduced to an army bed. He looked at it with displeasure. It was surely an odd sort of bed for a married man. How his father-in-law had been relegated to it he didn't know, but he suspected that the reasons were more or less the same as those for which he himself had made the move, and he couldn't entirely blame it on the children. After all, whether they had children or not, most married people slept in the same bed for years—no, for all their lives. It was something else. His working habits? He worked in his studio, which was in the house, next to his bedroom, till late into the night—sometimes till dawn—and got up late, so late he felt ashamed. Yet he had to get up late if he was to be bright when it mattered to be bright—during the night, when his wife and children slept, and the only sounds were those of the burner in the winter, and of the wind summer and winter. But he had kept such late hours even at the beginning of his marriage, and they had not prevented him—when his work was done, and a sort of numbness came over him that made him lay down his brush or pencil—from going to lie beside his wife on the double bed, close to her, his knees behind her knees, his feet behind her feet, his arms around her arms, as if they were about to walk into the night. Now, if at the end of his work he were to go over and move the children to make room for himself or rouse her and call her over to his bed, she would resist him—his embrace would meet her flailing arms. No, it wasn't the late hours he kept but something else, something that was at the roots of her nature and of his—in her, at all but the rarest times, an unconcealed shrugging away from making love as though it could give her only pain; in him, age-old, wearisome desire. Sometimes he went into her room, and if she wasn't reading the newspaper, which she often did for hours, he stood beside her bed and watched her fast asleep. Lying sidewise, half uncovered, one hand spread below her waist and the other clutching at her nightgown, whose folds gave her a fleeting, windswept look, she seemed like a pagan nymph afraid of getting ravished.

Once in a great while, he succeeded in drawing her to his room. She would come into bed with her dressing gown on. "Why should I make love? It's no pleasure," she said, one of the last times it happened, then sat, knees bent, and arms like a chain's link ringing her knees.

"Lie down, will you."

She finally lay down, still in her dressing gown.

"If you took off that overcoat, it would help."

"It's too cold."

"It's not a bit cold."

She sighed.

"Oh, stop sounding as though you were on the critical list all the time."

"We can't make love," she said, and laughed—laughed at him.

"Don't laugh. Why can't we? What's so strange about us?"

"It's you! It's you!" she said in a loud voice.

"Stop shouting at me. You're supposed to be loving me, not shouting at me."

"Oh, it's your fault," she said in a rage, and her thin, long arms, suddenly alive with strength, shook his heavy frame. "You are to blame."

"Other women don't complain."

"What other women?"

"You don't really think you are the only one?"

"Of course I am."

"Of course you are not."

"I don't believe you."

"What do you think I am? Some kind of monk?"

"There's no one else."

"Don't be so naïve."

"Who?"

"You don't believe me, do you?"

"No."

"Susan."

"Susan? You're fooling."

He wanted to say, "I am not fooling, and it wasn't anything like this," but a *frisson* had gone through her, and he didn't say anything.

"Of course you didn't make love to Susan," she said, but he could see that she believed it. "Not with Susan. She was so homely."

"She wasn't so homely."

She rose from the bed.

For a day or two, Susan, who had recently been a guest of theirs and had slept in the downstairs bedroom, seemed back in the house. Then at last he said, "No, I didn't really make love to Susan."

"I know you didn't," she said, and though she knew he

was lying, the lie comforted her. He had denied Susan; it was something that he had denied her. She would become one of those half-true, half-fictional characters about whom he himself hardly knew whether they existed more in real life or in his imagination.

Strange, he thought, that his wife should care so much about his relations with other women when she was so content to sleep alone. Or perhaps not strange at all. Ownership was the important thing—property; her interest was only stirred when someone was about to take him away from her, or borrow him for even a short while. Then, a peculiar intensity in her gaze, she quivered; then her eyes lighted and looked at him. But oh, that gaze, he thought. It was something to be gazed at like that by a woman. He responded. He could no more not respond than he could be spoken to and not answer. That gaze was his recompense—a sort of handout, which he accepted and was grateful for. Any other man would go, he thought—wouldn't stand for it one minute.

Again he looked at his bed, unmade, and made it, stretching the sheets tight and folding the corners in as he had learned to do so long ago he couldn't remember who had taught him. Some sergeant, was it, in the war? Very probably. If so, it went famously with the army bed. He tucked the blankets in with the same care. When he was a child, he remembered, he wasn't happy till he was tucked in so tight the sides of the mattress curled up like a hull and the covers formed a kind of deck. He slid into bed and switched the light out.

He recalled a verse that he had read, "Delighted and delighting like a bride," and laughed—in his mind only, of course. How very many things I go through the motions of only in my mind, he thought. Even painting is just a slight step beyond—tracing one's thoughts with a brush, color, or a pencil, the canvas only a step from nothingness. I am really at my best here in my thoughts while I lie still and silent. Definitely I am not a man of action. For every night that I don't sleep alone a hundred nights will pass in which I do. He turned over.

Only a few minutes had passed when he heard the door open, and a rustle, and in the half-light from the stairway saw his wife in her nightgown. "Well, what brings you here?" he said, switching on the light.

"Look," she said, holding out a page from the New York *Times.* "Here's a photo of a reproduction of this bed. Six hundred dollars. This is an original, so it's probably worth over a thousand."

"It'd be worth even more if you came into it."

"Oh, you can't think of anything else," she scoffed, and with a rustle of silk and paper went back to her room.

Having his studio at home, he hung around the house most of the day. At two o'clock, there was no sign of lunch. He strode into the kitchen. "Well, aren't we going to have lunch? It's two o'clock, you know."

"Oh, just make yourself a sandwich."

"Wonderful. We never see each other—not even at meals."

"We see each other all day. We see too much of each other. You're always around. Why don't you go out? Why don't you do something? I thought I was married to a painter."

"Oh, yes, you think it's so easy—just sit down and do a painting; turn them out like pots and pans. But I don't work like that."

"I'll say you don't. You work ten minutes a day. The rest of it you're around grumbling, complaining. No wonder I don't want to have lunch with you."

"I know, this is going to be just like your parents' house. God, I remember your father coming home from the office and nothing ready. I'd see him in the kitchen cooking himself some dinner. Pretty soon there won't be any supper here, either."

"Oh, you are the world's worst grump."

"Just like at your mother's and father's home, that's the way things are going to be."

"What are you talking about? My mother used to prepare meals all the time, except during the last years when she wasn't well."

"I see myself getting into your father's position more and more. I'm already sleeping in his bed. Well, you may be the image of your mother, but I am not like your father. I am not going to stand for it! What do you think!"

"I don't even know what you are talking about."

"His sleeping alone all the time. Don't tell me that went on just the last few years."

"Your parents slept separately, too."

"That doesn't mean *I* have to. I'm going to leave; I am not just going to wait and wait until I die."

"Why *don't* you leave? Go. I'm not holding you. But you aren't going to leave. If anyone is going to leave, it will be me."

"Why do you think I won't leave?"

"You'd miss us too much."

He was silent a moment. Perhaps she was right. He resumed complaining. It was easier, less consequential than threatening to leave. "Yes, if I don't do something, little by little the setup is going to be just like at your home. I remember one night when your mother was sick. I was sleeping in the sunroom, your sister was on the living-room sofa, and your father was sitting up in case your mother needed something. About three o'clock in the morning, your father was so tired he asked your sister to take over, and she said to him, 'Oh, no, you don't! You stay right there,' in a voice so harsh he didn't dare move, or even say anything. And she's always so gentle and sweet. I can just hear her talking to me that way—oh, not now, not this year or the next, but if she comes and lives with us, as she might, and gets more familiar with me, I can just hear her telling me off in that same voice."

"Oh, you are crazy. What do you want to eat?"

He looked down at the floor, slightly ashamed. As usual, he had said too much. "Oh, anything—whatever there is."

"Come on, Jennie," she said in a cheerful voice to their eldest daughter. "We're going to have lunch."

Later, he went up to his studio, paused in front of the canvas, and looked at it as if it were the most alien thing; he could not work. He wasn't always this nasty; when he could paint, when some strong idea gave him the energy to paint, his mood improved and he would go downstairs happily and play with the children or do some odd job around the house. Not today. Today he was without an idea, without energy, and he felt the pull of the bed drawing him like an undertow. He let himself go, dropped on the bed, and slept.

One day, two days, he was his beastly self. The third day, he must do something.

"I'm going out for a drive," he said to his wife. "I'll be out most of the day."

"I'm going, too," she said unemotionally. "My brother is coming this evening to pick me up."

"What?"

"I thought I'd go and stay in an apartment for a while."

"Are you joking?"

"No. I'll go with the children to my sister's, then look for an apartment."

He stared at her. Was she serious? He had known her to say things like this before and not mean them. Underplaying it, like a perfect Actors Studio graduate, she had been absolutely convincing every time, and every time he had fallen for it. He wondered. No, this time she really seemed to mean it. "Look," he said, "we could have your sister come here. We could . . ." He was quite beside himself with worry.

She was looking at him in a funny way—differently from before. He thought he could see a softening, the beginnings of a smile. "You don't mean it, do you?" he said.

"No."

"Why did you say it? Just to spoil my trip?"

"No," she said.

He left then, feeling at the same time exhausted and relieved, like one who has run a serious danger and escaped it.

The Room

"YOU should have seen him when he was a little boy,"
he once overheard his mother saying to a friend
about him. "He knew how I liked my room to be tidy, and
sometimes when I was ill in bed, if it got untidy, he would
say, 'Close your eyes, and don't open them till I tell you.'
Then, while I kept them closed and covered with my
hands, I would hear him running about the room putting
everything in order. 'All right, you can open your eyes
now,' he'd say. I would catch my breath to show him how
delighted and surprised I was, and he would stand there,
proud and beaming, his eyes bright as blackberries shining in the sun."

He remembered not just overhearing his mother but the
actual times she was referring to. He must have been eight
or so. Now, over forty, he went into the room, the same
room he used to tidy up for her, her room, which was hers
no more. She had named it "the pomegranate room,"
because of a pomegranate tree outside the window. Perhaps she had foreseen that the pomegranate would outlive her. It had. She was in her grave—had been for three
years. Sometimes a guest stayed in the room, or his
brother and sister-in-law. Though he would never use it,
when it was vacant he would go into it fairly often—just

open the door, switch the light on if it was dark, and stand there for a moment, surveying the emptiness, or, rather, her absence, for the room was fully furnished with the same furniture she had used. Even the books that had been read to her or she had read during her last illness were on the bookshelf, a few added and a few withdrawn. Hardly anything was missing; hardly anything had changed or been changed around. The walls were the same light ochre, with a few more spots and scratches, since they hadn't been repainted. Yes, the room was just the same as it had been ever since he could remember. "The same," he told himself, and almost smiled one of those smiles that have nothing to do with gladness but are the slightest movement of the lips—more like a sigh. In the silence he heard the air he blew out of his nostrils; its sound was as much as to say, "This is the way things are." Arms folded, he brought a hand to his chin and looked at the bed. The same bedcover. Not a crease. Nothing to straighten out. In the whole room everything in its place. Nothing to tidy up. If she were lying or sitting there, he couldn't help thinking, its looks could only please her. The room was a picture of neatness and order. He went out and closed the door behind him. There was nothing he could do. And anyway, as for neatness and order, she was past appreciating those qualities now.

Or perhaps she wasn't. How could one tell? Perhaps something of us lingered in the places we were familiar with, something of us, if only a memory. Perhaps memory was a living thing, a creature that we harbored in our brains, that lived in people's minds, ubiquitous, flaring now here, now there, clinging even to objects, extinguishing itself slowly, unwillingly, and having, like anything alive, its own wild urge to live, to be preserved. Perhaps no one was really dead till he was quite forgotten, till everything he knew was spoiled and shattered.

Her death was something he could not get over. Again and again he went into the room. What could he do? Everything was in such good order. Set flowers in the vase? "No, no," he told himself as he recalled the smell of the hundreds of flowers that had been brought to her room after her death. Their smell had clung to the room for days. A sickly smell. No—no flowers for an unlived-in room. She would have nothing useless. But there he went again, thinking of her wishes as though they mattered now.

Well, perhaps they mattered. And if so, what, what, indeed, would she like to have done to the room? If he could only do something that would make him as happy as the child he had been. He felt so far past the time when even by a simple thing joy was turned on full. He was sitting in the red armchair in the corner by the window. After a moment, he got up. Level with his eyes, two feet away, was the bookshelf, hanging from the wall. The books were all straight, none of them upside down, all set the way she liked them, neither too close to the edge of the shelf nor too far into it. He took a few steps, and his eyes settled on the spots, the scratches on the walls. Were there enough of them to justify painting the room over? He went around it like an inspector. Under the windowsill he found several scratches, several spots by the radiator; near the bed, the wall had been retouched with paint that did not quite match the old. The ceiling had several cracks and one large stain. Spirited now, some purpose in his eyes, he found more and more blemishes on the walls. He became happier with each new one that he saw. Yes, definitely the walls needed repainting. She had always loved fresh paint—to cover the past, the old, the soiled, the dusty, what had seen too much sickness, with something bright and fresh. He would paint it the same color but not quite, use tempera colors—her favorite—mix into the burnt sienna a tiny bit of red to catch the light of sunset.

With energy, with drive, he went into town and bought the chalk, the colors, and glue in a packet, and two brushes—one wide, one thin for the edges—and plaster for the cracks. Carefully, he mixed the paint, got the furniture out of the way, closed himself in the room, and started patching the ceiling, then painting. He painted with alacrity, the way he had tidied the room in his youth; only this took him not just a few minutes but two days. He put in all the hours he could spare. Nothing seemed more important. At last the room was done. The floor was made to shine, the furniture polished and put back, the books replaced.

"Well, it came out well, didn't it?" he asked one of the maids who had come for the spring cleaning.

"Yes, lovely," she said.

He asked another. "Yes, really looks good," she told him. Others, too, came to see it, and said how well it had come out. After they left, he went into the room alone. Looking at her bed, he could almost see her uncovering her eyes and catching her breath to show him her delight.

At the Dinner Table

"I THOUGHT we were going to be eight," Giacomo said to his wife, Jessie, seeing that she was setting the table for nine.

"Your father," she said.

"Do you really want him to sit with us tonight?"

"Yes, why not? He enjoys a little company."

"I know he enjoys it, but it's embarrassing. He's much better off in his room."

"No, he isn't," she said, and went on setting the table.

"I just hope he doesn't get one of those sneezing attacks. He doesn't know enough to leave the room. And then sometimes he just looks down, his chin against his chest, in a kind of stupor."

"Oh, not a stupor. Don't make things seem worse than they are. You should talk to him more."

"I think he should stay in bed. He dishes out his food to whoever's sitting next to him."

"A lot of people do that."

"And he keeps saying the same things all the time."

"So do you," she said, and laughed. "Try to be a little cheerful."

Giacomo's father, past eighty, was suffering from a variety of complaints, all probably owing to hardening of the arteries. His memory about recent events and names was almost gone. A little thing could move him to tears or, for that matter, though more rarely, to laughter. He walked unsteadily, with an odd gait, as if his center of gravity were ahead of him and he had to catch up with it in order to maintain his balance. He looked as frail as a leaf in the late fall. At times, he had fits of tremor. Certain problems seemed to elude his grasp; others, especially if they related to philosophy—his field—he was nearly as conversant with as he had been, and his critical abilities seemed almost unimpaired. And he could still read a lot, and make notes, though with a shaky hand.

That night, six paying guests were coming. The house, a large old villa near Siena, was being run partly as a *pension*. The guests were usually friends, or friends of friends. Giacomo's wife, an American, took care of the guests after his mother died.

It was mid-November. There had been guests earlier in the season, and in August the house had been almost full, but for the last few weeks no one had come, and now the household was in a rather high state of expectation. The cook had prepared a good meal. The small children would eat in the kitchen. The guests were American, two parties of them: one, a couple from New York; the other, a mother, daughter, and granddaughter, and an elderly lady friend. These arrived first, in a Jeepster driven by the elderly lady. "It has four-wheel drive," she said, squinting with satisfaction when complimented on it. The mother was in her fifties, the daughter in her thirties, the granddaughter about ten. They had never been to the house before but had heard of it through a relative, and the mother had written to reserve rooms long in advance. The letter said that her daughter had just been through a divorce and she was giving her this trip to Europe. As often is true in such cases, the two elder women seemed in much better spirits than the daughter, who looked wan, as if she were only physically in Europe, her mind still in Wichita, Kansas, where she came from. As for the granddaughter, she was pale and half asleep, and she showed the effects that a long journey over hilly country can produce on a delicate young frame. A daisy wilted by too much handling—that was how she seemed.

Giacomo and Jessie took them to their rooms, and for a moment Giacomo viewed the house through the guests' eyes—a maze of corridors, steps up and down, sharp corners.

"How will we ever find our way to the dining room?" the mother asked.

"A bell will ring, and we will come and fetch you. But it isn't too hard—the house is built around a central courtyard; well, no, two courtyards," Giacomo said, and he laughed.

The ten-year-old, like a seasick person setting foot on land, seemed to have revived, and as Giacomo left them and looked back from the end of a passageway, he saw her jumping back and forth, her left arm flexed, her right arm straight, as if she were fencing with an imaginary knight. Perhaps she thought she had come to a castle.

Then the second car arrived, with the couple from New York—she a wispy blonde, an ethereal, airy creature; he a large, practical-looking man, a surgeon. They had had trouble finding the house, had gone past it a few miles, and apologized profusely for being late.

"Oh, you are not late. Supper isn't quite ready yet," Jessie said.

"How d'you get into town from here?" the man asked. "We didn't go through it."

Giacomo tried to explain, then made several trips delivering luggage to the various rooms. He could see the surgeon wondering whether he should tip him. He retreated in haste.

The dinner bell rang, and in a little while everyone gathered around the table. Giacomo's father was last; all the others were seated when he arrived from his room adjoining the dining room. In a white, Indian-looking cotton jacket, something like a pajama top, and baggy gray flannels, he advanced warily. No one but Giacomo noticed him at first. Meekly, as if he didn't own the house but was an uninvited guest, he touched the back of his chair, and then Jessie saw him and introduced him. He begged for no one to get up, and sat down.

Now, Giacomo thought, he's going to try to get everybody's name straight, and, indeed, he began by asking the elderly lady on his right for her name, though she had just been introduced to him. Unable to remember it for even a few seconds, he drew a pad and pencil from his pocket and laboriously wrote the name down, and then those of her friend, her friend's daughter and granddaughter, and of the surgeon's wife. But unlike Giacomo—who thought, What a nuisance—they didn't seem to mind; they seemed amused. "And my husband's name is Alfred, if you want to write it down," the surgeon's wife said.

Giacomo's father declined with a slight, slow, oblique tilt of his head.

"The Signor is not interested in men's names," the surgeon said.

"Oh, you are not?" one of the women said.

Giacomo's father smiled, and everybody laughed.

Now he's going to ask them where they are from, Giacomo thought.

"And you are from . . . ," his father said.

"Wichita."

His father tried to pronounce the name several times, seemed to enjoy being corrected, said, "What a beautiful name—Indian, I suppose," and faithfully wrote it down, and Giacomo, though he was too far away to see it, knew exactly the fine pencil lines in the address book—minute, tremulous now, yet fairly clear, carefully made out. And when the surgeon's wife told him she was from New York, Giacomo knew what his father would say: "New York! Ah, the skyscrapers there seen from far away look blue as do mountains in the distance. In Chicago, they are scattered more at random, more chaotically than in New York." He had been to America on a lecture tour in 1951 and had come back with very strong impressions.

If only he weren't so predictable for me, Giacomo thought. "But then," he said to himself, "for them he isn't."

"All that tremendous weight of steel and concrete is made light if the building is beautiful," his father went on. "All its materiality is lost."

"Into spiritual lightness," the surgeon's wife, who was listening attentively, said.

"Yes," his father said, delighted with her response, and he looked at her intently, as if she were the chosen one. From that moment on, his eyes went back to her again and again in admiration, and Giacomo knew that his father wished she were sitting next to him; that he wished it keenly, almost painfully, and with all his heart, and that he loved her surely. "Yes," his father resumed, almost to himself, "of all the arts, architecture shows best this birth of spiritual lightness from material weight."

Ha, he hadn't given his father enough credit—this was something Giacomo had never heard him say.

The elderly lady was born in Los Angeles. Now he's going to say something about that, Giacomo thought. "Los Angeles is wonderful," his father said. "It goes over hills and valleys and mountains, from the desert to the sea. Infinite."

The conversation turned to Siena. "I asked your son how to get into town tomorrow morning. We got lost on our way here," the surgeon said, whereupon Giacomo's father said, "Oh," and left the table to go to his room. Giacomo knew exactly for what—a sheet of paper on which to draw a sketch of the way into town.

"I've already explained it to him," Giacomo said when his father returned and, putting the paper on the table beside the surgeon, leaned over and started drawing. But his father went right on with the sketch.

The surgeon said, "Oh, now I've got it. Yes, it's perfectly clear to me now—the mistake I made, I mean. We took a right there, at the level crossing, when we should have come straight on."

"Yes," his father said, pleased, and he returned to his chair with a faint smile.

"And we went beyond your drive," the surgeon said. "When I realized that we were lost, I stopped and asked directions of a motorcyclist standing by a store, and he turned around and led us to it. A couple of miles. The people are pretty nice around here."

"Yes, they are kind, especially here in the countryside."

Now about the oxen, Giacomo thought.

"When the farmers plow here," his father continued, "they speak or at most shout to their oxen; down near Rome, instead, they use a stick."

"Is that so?" the elderly lady said with great interest.

"Yes," Giacomo's father went on. "The Romans still show some of their old traits. They like knives, for instance. That, they say, explains the number of great surgeons they have had."

"Did you hear that, Al?" the surgeon's wife said.

Again they laughed.

[83]

"Do you manage to get into town once in a while?" one of the women asked him.

The question didn't seem to register with Giacomo's father, and Jessie answered for him. "He likes to go to the movies."

Now he's going to talk about American movies, tell us how much better they are than European. But his father merely said, "Lately I have been rather disappointed in the cinema."

He always ate more or less the same things: a plate of pasta and then croquettes. Because he preferred them, he thought they must be preferable to anything else that was served, no matter how elaborate, and so, as Giacomo had expected, he offered some of his food to the two women sitting beside him—didn't so much offer it as try to push it onto their plates. But the elderly lady didn't seem to mind at all. She accepted it and said the croquette was like a hamburger.

"Ha, hamburgers," Giacomo's father said, and related, as he often had before, how in America he had subsisted on them quite happily.

Now he lit a cigarette. He's going to sneeze, Giacomo thought, and at the moment of his thinking this his father closed his eyes and the sneezes came one after the other.

The woman on his left said with some glee, "You are allergic, like I am. The only thing to do is to take big breaths of fresh air. Come with me." She took him in charge as if he were a small boy and led him toward the window. He went with her gladly; she was a pretty, soft, rather buxom woman, with a pleasant smile. He seemed to take advantage of the little walk by clinging close to her, his arm in hers. She had him breathe deeply the fresh air from the partially opened window, and it worked. He returned with her, amid applause. "But, say, you are miraculous, a real healer," he told her.

"No, but I was a nurse once."

"And now I must retire," he said. "I go to bed early. I am old. If I miss the first sleep, it never comes again. Good night." Unsteady as he was, he knelt beside the lady on his left and kissed her hands; then he kissed the elderly lady on the cheek, then the other woman and Jessie lightly on the hair, and the ten-year-old, whom he also patted on the shoulder and said "dear" to; he touched his son, who returned the little gesture, and shook the surgeon's hand; and finally, more hesitantly, shyly, yet with a certain gleam in his eyes, he went to the surgeon's wife and kissed her, too. "Good night," he said to everyone. *"Buona notte,"* he repeated, waving his hand as he retreated toward the door.

"Your father's sweet," one of the ladies said.

"Oh, he is," said another.

"He's darling," the surgeon's wife said.

"You have a wonderful father," said the surgeon.

Giacomo's face brightened. He nodded. He certainly didn't want to be modest at his father's expense. He felt ashamed of having been ashamed of him. Why, he should be proud! He looked at the surface of his glass of wine as at a mirror and saw his image there. He thought of his fears that, like clouds, had now all dissipated. "You fool," he said to himself, and laughed.

"You see, your father didn't spoil the evening," Jessie said to him later, when they were alone.

"He saved it," Giacomo said.

The Soft Core

IT was suppertime. The bell had rung. Everyone was around the table except his father, nearly eighty. Sometimes he didn't hear the bell. So Giacomo went and knocked at his bedroom door.

No answer came. Going in, he found his father lying on the bed with his shoes on. His eyes were open, but they didn't seem to recognize Giacomo.

"Papa, dinner is ready."

"What? What is it?"

"Dinner," Giacomo said, without any hope now that he would come to it.

"Dinner," his father echoed feebly, making no effort to get up but rather trying to connect the word. Dinner where, when, his eyes seemed to be saying.

"You are not feeling well?"

"Yes, I'm well," he said, almost inaudibly. "I am well, but . . . you . . . you are . . . ?" His father could not quite place him.

"Giacomo. I am Giacomo," the son said.

His name seemed to make little or no impression on his father. Indeed, he seemed to have forgotten it already and to be groping for some point of reference, something familiar to sustain his mind, which was wavering without hold in space and time.

Quickly Giacomo stepped out of the room, through an anteroom, and opened the dining-room door. His wife, his sister, their children, and a guest were round the table eating, talking. He called his wife.

She rose and hurried over. "Is he all right?"

"No."

"Like last time?"

"No, no, not as bad."

They had in mind a time five or six months before, when Giacomo's sister had called from Rome for a phone number that their father had in his address book. Giacomo, then as now, had gone to call him in his room, and found him on his bed, unconscious, breathing thickly, and in a sort of spasm. A stroke, he thought. Thoroughly alarmed, he rushed back to the phone, hung up after a few hurried words of explanation, and called the doctor. In a few minutes, everyone in the house was round his father's bed. It seemed to Giacomo that the end had come. Its suddenness appalled him. He wasn't prepared for it. He had been so unfriendly to his father lately —almost rude. Why, only the day before, when his father had asked him to drive him into town, as he often did, Giacomo told him that he couldn't, that he was too busy, which wasn't really true. And other things came to mind —his curt replies to his father's questions, the long silences at table, and when there was some conversation, his father's being left out of it, ignored; his not laughing at his father's little jokes; not complimenting him on the fruit that came from trees he had planted, and for which he so much expected a word of praise when it was served at table. If Giacomo had only had some warning, to make up for his behavior—oh, he would have been his father's chauffeur, if he had known, talked with him about his books, his philosophy, his fruit trees, laughed at his jokes, listened keenly to the things he said and pretended it was the first time he heard him saying them. With a sense of anguish, he watched his father, unconscious, on the bed. He couldn't die just yet; he must talk again. The prospect that he mightn't—that he might live on paralyzed and speechless on that bed—was even worse.

They waited for the doctor. Yet, even before the doctor came, something might be done. He couldn't just wait and watch his father die in this awful, sunken state. To ease his breathing, Giacomo took out the dentures, which seemed to lock his father's mouth, and opened the window, because the radiator, going full steam, had made the room stiflingly hot. Then he hurried upstairs. In the drug cabinet, there were some phials of a relaxant—papaverine —that had once been prescribed for his father to help his circulation. Giacomo gave him two, by injection—a certain knowledge of medicine having remained from when he had studied it, and even practiced it, long ago—then waited for the effect. But even before the drug could possibly have had one, his father seemed to improve, to rise from his prostration. The breathing was easier. His limbs were slowly relaxing. It seemed that whatever had commanded them to stiffen was easing its hold, loosening up. His eyes began to look and not just gaze; the sounds coming from his mouth were not just moans but language, or the beginnings of it—monosyllables, bits with which words and phrases could be made. And the improvement was continuous. By the time the doctor arrived, he was moving his limbs and uttering words, though the words were disconnected. As the doctor examined him and prescribed treatment, his voice gained strength. He answered questions; he sat up; he even asked for food. An hour or two later, he was reading, making notes, pencil in hand

and postcard on the page, in case he should want to underline a word or a sentence that had struck him. And he looked very sweet there on the bed in his pajamas, reading under the light, thin and ethereal, all involved in that spiritual form of exercise. His body—the material aspect of it, his physique—which had been so much in the foreground and had so preoccupied them a few hours before, now seemed quite forgotten, back where it should be, something one is hardly aware of, that works better when one's mind is off it.

So his father had been given back to life, and Giacomo had another chance to be warm and friendly to him. At intervals that night, he slipped into the room to see how he was doing, or, if the light was out, afraid to wake him, listened outside with his ear to the door. Oh, this was easy enough to do, and it was easy to be solicitous the next day —ask how he was, and help him with the half-dozen drugs the doctor had prescribed, and with the diet. But when his father—well again, his usual self, full of the same old preoccupations and requests—resumed getting about and Giacomo heard his aged yet determined step coming toward his room, something in him stiffened as if in defense, and he waited for the door to open.

His father came in without a knock, as was his custom. "After all, cars now are pleasingly designed," he said in a slightly plaintive, slightly polemical voice, from just inside the doorway.

For a moment, Giacomo wondered what he was talking about. Then he remembered his father's arguing a few days before against an ordinance barring cars from the main street of the town. Giacomo had disagreed, and now his father was bringing the subject up again, bothered as always by anyone's disputing his viewpoint. "You like them?" Giacomo said.

"Well, they are certainly more pleasant to watch than

were carriages drawn by panting, weary horses. Besides, people put up with much more disturbing things than cars without complaining."

His father had his own peculiar ideas about traffic, about where Giacomo should park his car, about driving —about practically everything, in fact. He insisted on the frequent use of the horn, and if the person driving didn't blow it and he thought there was danger of a collision, he would shout to let the other party know that the car he was riding in was coming. It was almost as irritating as his bringing up an old argument and wanting to prove his point though a long time had passed. For him an argument was never closed. He went on pondering over it, debating it in his mind. One saw him doing it—wandering in the garden, pausing, starting to walk again, a true peripatetic —and if some new thought came to him he didn't hesitate to let you know it, wherever you might be.

About this matter of the ordinance, in the end Giacomo just nodded. Appeased, his father asked him for a favor. It was a way of showing he was on good terms with him. "Are you going into town tomorrow afternoon?"

Giacomo never planned his days ahead if he could help it. "Well, yes, I can go in, if you like."

"Would you? I need to buy some brown paper to line the crates of cherries with."

The cherries weren't ripe yet.

"Ah, yes, yes, I'll take you," Giacomo said.

"At about three o'clock?"

"The shops, you know, don't open until four."

"Say at half past three."

It took ten minutes to drive into town.

"Ah, yes, yes, all right."

Two or three times the next day, his father would remind him of the trip, and at a few minutes past three be at his door, ready to go. Giacomo would prevent himself from making any comments, but the very effort not to make them would keep him silent. "You are so silent," his father would observe in the car. "What is it?"

"Nothing. I am sorry."

"You have such a long face."

It was the hardest thing for Giacomo to look cheerful when he wasn't. He had no more control over his face than over his mood, and felt there was no poorer dissembler in the world than he. "I'm sorry if I can't be gayer," he would reply.

Sometimes his father would come into his room to ask him for advice on where to send an article he had written. But it seemed to Giacomo that he was asking for advice only in order to discard it. "I would send it to Wyatt, if I were you," Giacomo would suggest. But his father had already made up his mind whom to send it to, and it wasn't to Wyatt.

Speaking of his works, his father would say to him, "It is a *new* philosophy."

"Yes," Giacomo would reply, and be quite unable to elaborate. It was a pity, because his father yearned for articulate assent and recognition. People found his work difficult; some said they couldn't understand it. Nothing irked him more than to hear this. "Even Sylvia," he would say, referring to a guest, a pretty girl with a ready smile and pleasant manner, "who I don't think is very widely read in philosophy, found it clear." He never doubted that praise was offered in earnest. And no praise seemed more important to him than that which came from girls, from pretty women. Then a blissful smile would light his face and linger in his eyes.

With the single-mindedness of someone who has devoted his whole life to a cause, he gave or sent his articles around. He was so surely entrenched in his ideas that nothing could budge him from them. Each problem, each concept he came on had to be thrashed out and made known. Intent on it, if he met you—no matter where—he might stop and, pronouncing each word as if he were grinding it out, say without preamble, "Creativity is an underived, active, original, powerfully present, intrinsic, self-sustaining principle—something that cannot be resolved or broken up into preëxistent, predetermined data, and that is fraught with a negative possibility."

Giacomo would nod. He had been brought up to the tune of phrases such as these, had grown up with them, and though he had only begun to understand them he had finished by believing in them. At any rate, he was convinced there was a good measure of truth in what his father said. And yet he couldn't make it his own. "Negative possibility," *"causa sui,"* "psychic reality," "primal active"—these terms perplexed him. He knew they were full of meaning for his father, but he couldn't grasp it; it eluded him. They weren't in his language, and he looked on them with the detachment of one who looks on instruments he can never use.

The extraordinary importance his father gave his work! One had the feeling that nothing—not his wife, not his children—mattered to him quite so much as the vindication of certain principles. He probably saw his family, house, fruit trees, and philosophy as a whole—he had a unified view of everything—and felt that one could never damage the other; he probably even thought that his work was the key, the solution, to a host of problems, financial ones not excluded. Since he didn't teach and lived isolated in the country, to advance his views he tirelessly went to the post office to send off his manuscripts and books, as well as reprints of his articles, which he ordered by the hundreds. He sent them assiduously, and impatiently he waited for acknowledgments and answers that often failed to come.

It was all very admirable, but Giacomo couldn't really admire it. He was more inclined to admire his mother, who painted and often hid her paintings in a cupboard. He thought of some of the landscapes she had done, particularly one of a row of vines, a study of green done with such love of leaf and branch and sod and sky its value couldn't be mistaken, yet, because his father—perhaps with a slight frown or tilting of his head—told her it was not among her best, she had put it in a cupboard, and it had never been framed until after her death. Paintings, his father said, looked better unframed. "Let's wait till we have a bit more money before buying one," he would say, which meant never to everyone but him.

His father wrote and spoke about the value of spontaneity in art and literature and all things, but was he spontaneous? He seemed the opposite to Giacomo sometimes—very deliberate and willful. And how he wanted to escape his father's will. He still felt it upon him as he had when he was a child, a boy, a young man. His father's will shaping his life. His brother's life, too. At school, his brother had been good at all subjects, including mathematics, so his father must have a scientist in the family and had strongly advised him—and wasn't advice, especially the advice of someone whom you admired, harder to disobey than a command?—to study physics and mathematics at college, subjects for which he had no special gift. His brother hadn't, as a result, fared well at college. And as for Giacomo, when he was twenty-two and had been away from home, overseas, for seven years —it was wartime—his father had written, making it seem urgent that he come back immediately. "You are coming home to save your mother," one of his letters said. And Giacomo, who would have wished to delay his return another year—there was a girl, there were his studies, well begun—had gone back only to find that his father had exaggerated, sort of been carried away.

Then his father had a way of asking Giacomo to do things that instinctively made him wish to disobey. He seemed to like asking favors, to ask them for the sake of asking. Giacomo had never answered a flat no; he wasn't that familiar with his father. Recently, though, he had done something worse. His father had called to tell him once again about a cistern whose drainage had become a fixed idea with him. Giacomo had made the mistake of contradicting, and now his father, pencil and paper in hand, came after him so he would get a thorough understanding of his plan. But Giacomo, who had heard enough of it, went off, leaving his father in a rage. Never before had he refused to listen. Now, doing so, he experienced a strange sense of freedom, as though he had shaken off the bonds of childhood. For a moment, he felt almost snug and comfortable in his attitude toward his father. Perhaps it wasn't all unjustified, he thought, and old, childhood resentments came back to him. He remembered a fall from horseback when he was a boy: limping home, with a gaping wound about the knee that needed stitching, his father scolding him for it, and the words of his mother—soothing, like something cool upon a burn—and her taking him to the hospital, the doctor telling her it might be better if she left the room, her replying that she had once been a nurse, staying with him, holding him by the hand while the doctor put the stitches in. His father had scolded him, instead. No, he thought, perhaps I am not altogether in the wrong.

But seeing his father watch the sunset in the garden as he so often did, absorbed in light, a man whom beauty had always held in sway, or hearing him recite a poem—though now he rarely did—enunciating the words in all their clearness, slowly, in a voice that seemed ever on the verge of breaking yet never broke and that seemed to pick each nuance of rhythm and of meaning, Giacomo felt his old love, respect, and admiration come back full to over-flowing as when he was a child and it seemed to him that his father never could be wrong—in the realm of the spirit, a man of mighty aims and wider grasp.

And chancing to meet him late at night going into the kitchen for food, looking so frail and thin in his pajamas and so old without his dentures, Giacomo felt ashamed of himself. Oh, his unfriendliness was revolting. That he should be distant and cold toward his father now when he was weak and wifeless, now when he was so old he had become almost childish in some ways—laughing and crying with ease. It was unforgivable, horrible, inhuman. If it hadn't been for his father, where would they be, Giacomo asked himself. If his father hadn't taken his family out of Italy in time, they might all have perished in a German concentration camp. And he had seen that his children learned English almost from babyhood. And he had never raised a hand against them. And he had been generous with those who needed money or lodging or employment.

Well, there was nothing for it but to change his attitude. He must make more of an effort. No week went by without Giacomo's telling himself this. He would talk to his father as to a friend, about any subject that came to his mind. "What this town needs, I think," he said to him at lunch one day, trying to be nice, "is a newspaper. I'd like to start one."

"It would be a very bad idea," his father said.

"Why?"

"But it's obvious why," his father snapped with irritation and perhaps even dislike.

"Well, I wish you would explain it."

"But anyone can see that if there were only one news-paper in the country it would have a better chance of being a good one."

This wasn't like his father at all. He seemed only to want to contradict.

"I thought that to encourage writers and the arts, as well as trade, a local paper . . ." Giacomo didn't finish his sentence. Why should he? His father's face seemed full of aversion, as though Giacomo were saying something blas-phemous.

The meal went on in silence. Giacomo looked up at his father. The lines of his face were still set in anger, and he was looking down at his plate, the segment nearest to him, almost at his napkin. No, one could not change, Giacomo thought. His father could not change. He him-self could not change. Perhaps if one could fall into a state of oblivion one could change, but otherwise?

And then came the evening when his father did not turn up for supper and Giacomo went to call him in his room. It wasn't nearly as bad as the earlier time, when he thought his father had had a stroke—after all, now he was conscious, his breathing was normal, he wasn't in a spasm, and he could speak. Yet Giacomo had the same feeling that the end had come. His father seemed so tenu-ously, so delicately attached to life, like down of a thistle in the wind. And when he spoke he was like a flame that wavered in the air this way and that, sometimes almost detached from the body that fed it.

It seemed as though he were living in another century and in another land. "We'll have to ask the Byzantine government," he said.

"What Byzantine government?" Giacomo asked.

"In Constantinople," his father replied, as if he found

it odd for anyone to ask a question with such an obvious answer.

It was strange he should speak of the Byzantines. His father's ancestors were from Venice, and Giacomo sensed that his father was talking of the affairs of six or seven centuries ago.

To bring him back to this one, he began to speak to him, to explain just what had happened and to reassure him. He told his father that his memory would all come back to him in a little while, after he had drunk some coffee. And he went on to tell him who he was, and, when his wife appeared with a cup of coffee, who she was, and about the house, his fruit trees, his articles and books, the recent letters; he went over all his life with him, in a fashion.

Intent on reconnecting himself to the past and those around him, patiently, like someone threading beads, the present not quite with him, his father sat up on the bed and, speaking very gently, asked him questions. "Where is Mama?" he said, referring to his own wife.

For a second, Giacomo didn't answer. He had expected and feared the question. Then he said, "She died. You know, she died three years ago."

"Ah, yes," he said sadly, and for a moment father and son seemed not so much to look at one another as to survey the last days of her life.

"And you say we went to England?"

"Yes, do you remember, in 1938? You took us there."

"Yes. You children were so good on that crowded train."

"And when we got to England you saw a sign that read, 'Cross at your own risk,' and you said it was worth coming just to see that sign, and that in Italy it would have said, 'It is severely forbidden to cross.'"

His father smiled. "It was a sign of freedom."

"Yes."

"And then we came back here?"

"Yes, by boat, after the war. The bailiff met you in Naples, all the money he had for you stuffed under his garters, in his socks. He was afraid of thieves."

They laughed together. Laughter, it has the power to reconcile lost friends, to bridge the widest gaps.

"Your wife . . . tell me her name again."

"Jessie."

"Ah, yes, so dear," he said tenderly. He got up slowly and went to his desk for a pencil. He said he wanted to write the name down before he forgot it once more. He looked at the desk aimlessly, then pulled out the wrong drawer. "My little things," he said, "where are they?" He looked like a child whose toys a gust of wind has blown away.

Giacomo found a pencil for him, and his father wrote the name Jessie on a piece of paper. Next, he paused by the bookcase. All the books in it he had annotated, but now he looked at them as if for the first time.

"This one you wrote," Giacomo said.

His father looked at it closely. "This one I know. But the others . . ." He stroked his head as if to scold it. "And these are your poems," he said, seeing a flimsy little book with his son's name. "I remember the first one you wrote, about the stars, when you were ten. Strange, your mother's father, too, wrote one about the stars—his best one."

"You see, you remember a lot."

"About the distant past. Such a long time . . . for you, too." He smiled, then, looking at him warmly, said, "Our Giacomo," and it was as it had been when Giacomo was a boy and his father used to look at him and say "Ajax," because he considered him generous and strong.

Strangely, now, Giacomo found that he *could* talk to his father, easily, affably, and with pleasure, and that his voice was gentle. When his father was well, he couldn't, but now he was reaching the secret, soft core—the secret, gentle, tender core that is in each of us. And he thought, *This* is what my father is really like; the way he is now, this is his real, his naked self. For a moment it has been uncovered; he is young again. This was the young man his mother had met and fallen in love with; this was the man on whose knees he had played, who had carried him on his shoulders up the hills, who had read to him the poems he liked so much. His other manner was brought on by age, by a hundred preoccupations, by the years, by the hardening that comes with the turning of the years.

Already, with coffee, with their talk, his father was recovering his memory. Soon he would be up and about, and soon Giacomo wouldn't be able to talk to him as he did now. But though he wouldn't, he would think of his father in the way he had been given back to him, the way he had been and somewhere—deep and secret and only to be uncovered sometimes—still was.

The Bell

HE thought, I must live like a poet, and at this moment that means bearing with him.

It was three o'clock in the morning, and his father—eighty-two, helpless, bedridden, and with his mind wandering—had rung the bell again.

"He was born with a bell in his hand," the son said to himself. It was what his mother used to say about some people, her husband and daughter not excluded. His mother was dead now—had been dead six years—but her son still saw her, still heard her. A thousand things in the house, an old country house in Tuscany, summoned her to his mind. His mind was always open to her, eager for her.

He groped for the light cord. The bell in his bedroom was on another cord, thinner, smoother, of fine, frayed cotton, and it ended in a wooden, pear-shaped switch, almost an antique. Like his mother, the son never rang a bell, and this perhaps accounted for its not having been replaced with a little plastic knob like those in most of the other rooms. Even if he did ring, there was no one to answer—no live-in maids or cook, as there had been. The huge house had a bell in almost every room, and downstairs, near the kitchen, a board on which different numbers popped up when the bells were rung. Only a few still worked—the front door, his father's, and two or three others, but no one knew for sure to which rooms they belonged. Erratically, these popped up like naughty marionettes, even when no one had rung, and when they were cancelled they could not be trusted to stay down.

He switched on the light and drew his legs out from the warm covers into the chilly air. It was winter, and though this part of the house was heated, it was never really warm. The coal fire in the furnace burned full blast for only a few hours after it was lighted. During the night it died down, to be relit the next day by a handyman who had been with them twenty years and who lived nearby with his family.

He got into his dressing gown and slippers, and undertook the small journey to his father's bedroom, directly beneath his own, along cold brick corridors, the stone staircase, through the tiled telephone room, the dining room, and an anteroom. The light was on under his father's door.

"What is it?" the son said, peeking in.

"How do you mean 'What is it?' You are so curt."

"You rang the bell."

"But most certainly I rang the bell."

"Well, what do you need?"

"What do I need!" his father said irritably. "Come in and shut the door. Close that shutter, will you?"

The son walked to the middle of the room. "But it's shut. The shutter's shut. It doesn't need closing."

"But it does—can't you see?" Frail, slight except in his bones and eyes, his father was sitting up in his bed, which was set in an alcove of the room, looking at him with brows knitted.

The son walked over to the window. It was closed tight, and so were the inside shutters that fitted into the casements. Only, on the right-hand shutter the little bolt hadn't been pushed all the way under its bracket. He moved it over. "Is that better?"

"Oh, bravo," his father said, and now he seemed perfectly happy. "Tell me, what time is it? I can't find my watch."

"It's right there beside you, on the table. It's just past three o'clock."

"Three o'clock?" his father said, aghast. "Three o'clock in the afternoon?"

"No, it's night. Three o'clock at night."

"Night?"

"Of course. See," the son said, opening the window wide. The perfumed night entered the lighted room, and a rectangular light was cast upon the garden. "It's dark."

"But that doesn't make it three o'clock."

Strange, the playful way he reasoned. "Your watch," the son said sternly, not acknowledging the joke.

His father put his glasses on and picked up the watch, as if he still was not convinced. "So it is," he said. "Three o'clock." After a moment's thought, he added, "But I must go to the ceremony."

"What ceremony?"

"How do you mean 'What ceremony?' " his father said sharply. "The ceremony, of course. . . . The funeral."

"Whose funeral?"

"My funeral."

"Why, you haven't died."

"I haven't died?" his father said, looking about the room as if following a bat's flight. "I haven't died, you say?"

"No, and you are not about to. You'll probably outlive me!"

"You may not reach my age, but I won't outlive you," his father said, surprising the son with his reasoning.

"Who knows!"

"But how can you say that when I am dead already?"

"You are speaking. Your heart is strong. You have a good appetite."

"I didn't eat anything."

"There's the tray with your empty dishes. You've eaten everything up."

"Is it possible? It's true it seems that way, but it isn't."

"Oh, Papa. You must try and sleep now. It's late. So late it's almost morning, and I am sleepy; I must go to bed."

"Yes, you go now."

"Good night."

"Good night."

Slowly the son made his way up the stairs back to his room.

In the room adjoining the son's bedroom, two of his children slept soundly, and, two rooms over, so did his wife with their youngest child. He slept in a room of his own because of his father's calls and in the hope of doing some work. From a distance he viewed the sketches on his desk, at which he didn't manage to sit much anymore. He took off his dressing gown, slumped into bed, and put the light out. He waited for the bell to ring again. He was sure it was going to—positive. Yet if he waited perhaps it wouldn't ring. Perhaps his waiting for it, his expecting it to ring, was the one thing that kept it from ringing. So he hung on to wakefulness, sure that the moment he closed his eyes and fell asleep the bell would ring. And, indeed, it did, for sleep had stolen over him. He uncurled himself. He might just ignore this peal. But there came another— long, insistent. He rose and went down once more to his father's room.

"Yes?"

"Where am I?"

"Here in your home. Try not to ring the bell so often."

"There you are, rebuking me again."

"I am not rebuking you. You can't sleep. Let me give you something." He went to the medicine cabinet and took out a sleeping pill and a tranquillizer, then half filled a glass of water from a pitcher on the table. "Here, these will let you rest."

His father looked at the pills suspiciously. "What are they?"

The son told him.

Still his father gazed at them. Could he trust his son? He glanced up quickly, then back at the pills, seeming to weigh them. He had always been against sleeping pills. He didn't want to rely on them for sleep. But now he wasn't on his feet anymore, and the days went by listlessly, one after another, and he slept to make time pass —time that alone could bring the improvement he still hoped for.

"Take them, or you won't sleep."

His father put the pills in his mouth and swallowed them with the water, but not before he had caught a taste of them, as the son saw from the embittered face.

"Perhaps you'd like a little apricot brandy."

"Oh, that, yes."

He poured his father and himself each a tiny glassful from a bottle he took from a shelf in the bookcase, and watched his father drink it like a balm.

"A drop more?"

"Yes, yes. It's the best I've ever tasted."

The son told him it was Bols—Dutch—and his father tried to bring to the surface of his mind the names of his favorite liqueurs. With the son's help, he was able to recover one or two.

Carefully, his hand trembling, yet without spilling a

drop, as if it were something very precious, after a few sips his father set the little glass on the bedside table.

"Good, well then, good night," the son said, and rose to go, pleased to leave his father in a better mood than he had found him in.

"Good night. Take care you shut both doors." His father meant the one of the anteroom, too.

"All right."

He had shut the bedroom door when the bell's ringing stopped him short, and he turned to open it again. "What now?" he said, unable to hide a note of irritation and destroying the mood the brandy had engendered.

"I'm sorry," his father said in a meek, small, embarrassed voice that put the son to shame. "I meant to switch the light off and pressed the bell instead."

"The bell is that one," the son said, pointing to it.

"That one?" his father said, pointing to the light switch.

"No, that one. The smaller of the two. It's much smaller, you see."

"So it is." His father switched the light off.

"Well, good night."

"Good night."

That night, there was no further call.

"He rang three times last night," the son told the maid in the morning. She was the wife of the handyman, very plain and quiet. At first sight, or when she answered the telephone, she seemed gruff, but the gruffness was just a coating—the more you knew her the more you admired her. She was absolutely reliable, patient, sensible, and always doing things, so that the children, especially his younger girl, followed her everywhere, helping her put the rooms in order, or shell peas, or gather grass for her rabbits.

"Now he's sleeping," she said. "I looked in."

She looked after his father during the day, but at night she went home.

Besides mistaking it for the light switch, sometimes his father forgot to ring the bell, forgot there *was* a bell, or could not find it, though it hung within easy reach by the wall. The son bought him one of a different kind—not a bulb hanging on a cord, like the light switch, but a disc with a button—and he attached it to the wall, hoping this measure would avoid confusion. It helped, but still his father had difficulty. At such times, after fumbling in the dark for God knows how long, he would give up and shout. His voice was so loud it would fill a good part of the house, and it seemed louder for the silence that reigned there during the night. They were a long way from town and quite a distance from the road—a minor one, at that. For the son, the volume of his father's voice was a pretty accurate indication of his health, and a weak voice worried him more than a loud one. Still, it was even more compelling than the bell, and eerie, too, this tearing of the silent night. He would rush down, hoping not to find his father on the floor.

"Oh, at last," he would be greeted in an angry voice. "Why don't you ring the bell?"

"The bell . . . the bell," his father replied, trembling with irritation. "Where is it?"

"There!"

"You have all abandoned me. I am dying."

"With that voice?"

"Oh, heaven! You—who are you?"

"Your son," he replied, thinking his father had forgotten, but he had asked in anger, not in confusion.

"You don't behave like my son."

"It seems to me I come down when you call."

"Reluctantly."

"Well, you know, it's not exactly fun. What is it that you wanted?"

"What is it that I want indeed! Everything. I am in want of everything. I am left all alone." He seemed to have forgotten what he had called for. "Do me a favor," he said after a moment. "Get me Leopardi's poems. It should be there on the desk. I can't walk."

"Yes, of course; I know." On the desk there were three piles of books, mostly poetry. The son went through them hastily. "No, it's not there."

"But it must be."

He went through them again. Nothing. "I'll look in the bookcases." No, it wasn't in the bookcases, either.

"Look, there on the desk," his father said, his voice rising.

Why did his father always make him feel like a child with his orders, a child with none of childhood's advantages and all its disadvantages, as if nothing but submissiveness were expected of him? He expected the son to be so submissive. Yet why? He was only asking for a book. "I looked," he said.

"Oh, Lord! There in the first pile."

The son looked again, more carefully. Sure enough, the book was there, at the bottom. "Oh, yes, you're right. Here it is." It amazed him how often his father was right and he wrong.

"Thank you," his father said, and the son thought, He's never petty, never says "I told you so"; he never even says "You see." His father took a pencil, put his glasses on, and began reading.

The son watched him and felt he wasn't wanted anymore. He should ask his father to read a poem, for he loved reading aloud to people. And then perhaps he could read something to his father. But he felt unable to do either thing—unable to humor him. It was like an impediment. He remembered lying on that bed as a child, and his father reading poetry to him. Once, when his father was reading the *Iliad,* the stove in the corner of the room (it wasn't lit now, since there were radiators) had got hotter and hotter. Its red-hot pipe had ignited the ceiling and a flame had leaped out. From the bed he had seen it and given the alarm. His father had put the fire out with pails of water and then praised him for saving the house. And once, listening to him read Dante, the son had fallen asleep on that bed. Now the positions were pathetically reversed. Slowly, he left the room.

His father didn't like him—the son could sense it. Oh, he had loved him then, when he was a child, and again much later—fairly recently, in fact—when, away in America, he had translated some of his father's articles into English. But they had reached another stage. Though his father's memory was defective, his sensitivity was unimpaired, even heightened maybe. It was as if, having lost one faculty, the mind tried to rely more heavily on the others, or the others came to the help of the stricken one. His father resented the son's curt replies, his hurry to leave the room, his inability to be affable and keep him company. But his son couldn't change; hard though he tried to, he couldn't. It was the most difficult thing, he thought, to change one's attitude toward another person, or even to dissemble. He could only do it for a few minutes at a time by reminding himself constantly, constantly checking and controlling himself.

"Why so hostile?" his father would say. And, "You don't love me anymore? What have I done? Tell me."

The questions, often coming right after he had washed his father, changed him, or lifted him onto a chair, left the son nonplussed. "Why, why do you say that? Haven't I just . . ."

He felt powerfully that it was his duty to stay in the house and look after his father, but he couldn't do it graciously. He wasn't a good nurse. With an unlimited amount of money, he might have been able to hire one, but, as things were, no, he couldn't get the ideal nurse—not for twenty-four hours a day. For a time, he had had an old orderly. It had worked for only a matter of weeks. His father had grown more and more impatient with the poor old fellow, and finally he had left. The son's wife helped. Indeed, his father often said she was an angel. But she had her three small children to look after, and at night she was too tired to get up. So at night now the son was responsible, and often during the day, too, when the maid, who was over sixty, couldn't come. Just recently, she had been away for three weeks with a bad case of influenza. The idea of sending his father to a nursing home sometimes crossed the son's mind, but he wouldn't do it. Let him die in peace in his own house, where he wanted to be. He had had a bout with an old folks' rest home, and he had almost died there. It had happened a year before, when the son was in America. His father had fallen in his room at night and been found in the morning on the floor. At the hospital, they took one small X-ray, read it as negative, and dismissed him. Because he was unable to walk, he was put in the rest home, and there he stayed for three weeks, until the son flew back and took him home and called a specialist. There was a fracture indeed, but with his father in such critical condition an operation was thought inadvisable. Slowly, over a period of months, he had pulled out of that crisis.

Sometimes his father wouldn't call the son but would get up unaided and, if he didn't fall, would lift himself onto a chair—though not always the wheelchair—and, if he didn't get stuck, and if, in fact, he had got onto the wheelchair, would push himself along toward the door, open it, and cross the anteroom, the dining room, the telephone room, a corridor, and reach the kitchen, open the refrigerator, and then, if he didn't find what he wanted, shout.

The son, a light sleeper, would almost always hear him, and, hurrying down, ask his father why he hadn't rung the bell.

His father, convulsed with anger, would hardly be able to reply. But some words broke out. "Why, why, why! Isn't it obvious why?"

The vast house—practically empty, and with the old man in the bare kitchen, pale, in a wheelchair, chiding his son in the cold, still night—seemed a place to run away from. And it had been so happy once, when his mother was alive and he and his brothers were children. Later, too. It could be so now again—his wife, his children were upstairs—if only there was no sickness. If only his father could get well. But there was no chance of it. And, unworthy yet insistent, the thought came to his mind: if only his father were to die! But his father wouldn't die; he clung to life obscenely. The son hated himself for thinking so, for saying these words to himself, and yet he felt them. That's the way he felt deep down—oh, not even so deep down; the feeling was all through him, and it frightened him.

To hear his father even if he didn't ring or call, the son set up an intercom between his father's room and his own. Now he could hear his father's breathing, his soliloquies, his endeavors to rise, his talking in his dreams, his groans —more than anything else, his groans—and he thought of the "Ode to a Nightingale":

The weariness, the fever, and the
    fret
Here, where men sit and hear each
    other groan

Often a sigh would come through, a long sigh that seemed
final, the end, but always it was followed by another.

Sometimes there would be a crisis. His father would
take no food, his voice would thin, become a reed of a
voice. Just enough of a voice to ask for a glass of water
and announce in a prophetic tone, "Tonight I will die; this
is my last night with you," and though the son had heard
him say those words before, it was hard to disbelieve that
thin reed of a voice and that prophetic tone. His father
was so convinced of what he was saying, as though there
were no question. Then the son would keep vigil in his
father's room, and when he finally left he would go in the
drawing room and sit alone on the yellow sofa and wait
confidently. But when, hours later, on tiptoe, he would
reach the bedroom door and, like a thief, open it without
a sound and listen, he would hear his father breathing
hard.

The crises came irregularly every few weeks. There
were so many things wrong with his father: the fractured
hipbone that hadn't been set, his mind that wandered, a
cough, incontinence, and lately, as if that wasn't enough,
a peptic ulcer. But his heart was strong, its beat regular,
and it kept him alive. And his eyes were good—he could
read; his hearing was perfect. There was this to be said for
nature: it provided you with so many faculties that no
matter how many were struck out some were left intact.
He read poetry mainly, often aloud to visitors and to the
maid. She sat with her hands clasped on her lap, looking
at him, and listened, as at church, quite contentedly. The

children would come to him. Not all of them—the oldest
one didn't like going into a sick old man's room, but the
smaller ones didn't mind, particularly the little girl; she
would go and see him and give him her hand and stand
beside his bed and not be afraid to kiss him.

Weathering each storm, still his father clung to life. "Is
life worth living in that state? I say it is not," the maid
would say, and dutifully bring him milk and soup, and
tend him as if life were in fact very worth living, even in
his case—in no matter whose case. But the son, sometimes
—seeing his father restless, fretful, and not improving but
rather worse in practically every sense—counting the
drops of laudanum or picking out pills of a soporific,
would add one or two to the usual dose. In three-quarters
of an hour, his father would sink into a deep sleep. Late
in the morning, the maid would come to ask if she should
wake him up. "No, let him sleep," the son would answer,
and secretly hope his father would not wake.

Always he would wake up, refreshed and feeling better,
around noon.

To kill a man you had to give him five times the usual
dose—not just one or two drops more but eighty or a
hundred. It was easy enough to give a few drops more, but
a hundred—it would be like pulling a trigger. Beyond
him. Quite beyond him. Let his father die in his own time.
As for himself, he could wait; he could leave.

But seeing his father losing hope in his improvement,
dissatisfied with the doctors, and rising out of one crisis
only to meet another, again the son would wonder.

"What is death like, I wonder," he asked his father one
such time.

"I've seen it, death. I have," his father answered, his
head reclining on the pillow and looking at the ceiling, as
if speaking of someone he had met. "It is a dim gray ward
in which your senses fade little by little."

And his son thought, This is the true picture. And, He's perfectly right not to want to die. He has seen death, knows it from close by, has seen its gorge, knows just what it is like. And the son thought of the orange eye of a cat gone opaque and dull, the eardrum become sodden, the tongue unwieldy, the skin numb, everything powerless, flaccid, or worse than flaccid—stiff. From that time on, he didn't increase the dosage, not even by one drop, and though before he had wished—hoped—for his father's death, he didn't now, and he remembered his father's saying long ago, "Better to be the last among the living than the first among the dead." No, let him live on, outlast the son if need be. He seemed a leaf of last year still hanging to the tree, a leaf that no wind could blow off. The storm would come that would take him, but it had to be a hurricane. The son waited for it, and hated himself.

It came, a great crisis. For days his father wouldn't eat; his voice weakened to a thread. "This time there's no return," the maid said, shaking her head. The son phoned his sister and one brother. They came. But by the time they arrived their father had begun taking a little milk. Soon he was talking again.

"He has this terrific resilience. I'm sorry I alarmed you," the son said to his brother and sister, and they left.

In the spring, the old cook came—not much younger than his father. She had been with the family for forty years. Recently she had spent the winters with her daughter and grandchildren some two hundred miles north. His father had asked for her again and again, and she had returned to be with him.

Heavy, buxom, talkative, her hair dyed black, each morning she knocked gently at his door or looked in if he was asleep, and answered cheerfully each of his calls, and cheerfully brought him breakfast, washed him, powdered him, joked with him, told him stories, held his hand. For a while, he seemed to improve; then there was another relapse. But in the summer he was often well enough to be wheeled out into the garden in his chair.

And now it was mid-August. September—the real beginning of the year, the month in which people move and take up new positions—was at hand. In the spring, the son had been offered a teaching job in America. He had accepted it, thinking that surely in September his father would not be alive. But he was, and should he leave him in the care of two old women? His father might live on and on. The son couldn't tie himself down indefinitely. He went.

In October, while he was in his office, he received a call from his wife. A telegram had come saying his father was in a coma. I won't fly over, he thought. There's nothing I can do. He waited. For two days there was no news. Perhaps he's got over it, he thought. Then, on the third day, he phoned home, and his little daughter answered. "Nonno died," she said.

"He did?"

"Yes, a telegram came; Nonno died."

"On Wednesday," his wife said. It was Friday now.

So it was all over. The hurricane had come. The leaf had been severed. The son thought of his mother and his father. He wanted to remember them as their lithe and graceful selves, and instead he remembered them mainly in their agonies. Why did death take such a giant toll of one's memories? Death haunted him, stalked him.

Days later, letters arrived from the two old women in Italy. "He went like a candle," one said. "We said good night to him, tucked him in, and he never woke up."

The night from which his father did not wake, the night that for him was forever night—the son wasn't there. Did he wish he had been? He hardly knew. But he knew it was right, fitting, proper that he had been excluded. With the bitter, acrid taste of heartburn, his curt replies came back to him, his silences when affableness was needed, his cheerless manner. They were far better company, those two old women. Long, long ago, he had ceased to be a poet, perhaps had been one only as a boy.

Last Days

W HERE'S my love?" Giacomo heard her say as she
stepped into the garden from the drawing room.
She said it in Italian—*"Dov'è il mio amore?"* pronouncing
the word with an open "o" (she was from northern Italy),
and it sounded awful to his Tuscan ears, almost like a
sacrilege of love. Perhaps he wouldn't have minded so
much had he not known her. But he knew her all too well:
Leonora, a friend of his sister's. Forty—about his age—
and, like him, married. His sister, Clara, had brought her
on a visit here the year before, and from the start she had
given him no peace. "I've been wanting to meet you for
years; you're famous," she'd said. He had made a small
name for himself with his paintings, but he wasn't famous, and the hollow praise made him cringe. His wife's
presence notwithstanding—she and the children, who
now were in America, had been here with him then—
Leonora openly began making advances to him. She re-
minded him of the picture of a woman on a cigar box he
had seen—glossy, black curly hair; broad, avid smile; red
lips; bosomy. Some might have considered her good-
looking, as she certainly did herself. Speaking of her
daughter, she said, "She's not like me. She's like her father. I am beautiful. She's not." He liked subtle, delicate

women. This one was lusty, enterprising, proud. "Come for a walk with me," she had said to him only a few minutes after they had met. He shied away from such boldness and said no.

"Why not? Are you afraid I'll eat you up?"

He looked at her heavy jaws, her wide red lips. "Yes," he replied, and laughed.

"How stupid you are," she said to him.

He wasn't used to being called stupid, and he turned away.

"Come on, Giacomo, don't be offended. You are not offended, are you? Come for a walk." Life for her was a playful hunt; he wondered just how playful.

He thought of his lonely nights—he and his wife were not getting along—of the single bed in his room downstairs, and he turned back to her. "In a while, perhaps," he said.

She nodded, satisfied—gloating, almost, with satisfaction.

He met her in the front yard later in the afternoon. "Shall we take our walk?" she said. "You promised."

"Well, all right," he said. "Where shall we go?"

"You have some woods around here?"

"Yes," he said, "that way."

She was very inquisitive about what sort of relationship he had with his wife, and in the woods—once they got there and found a pretty place in which to sit—she chided him for looking at the trees and not at her. "Look at me," she said, and with both hands turned his face toward her. "You don't love me? I love you." The statement evoked no joy. It was an expression more of will than of love and only firmed his aloofness.

He got to his feet. "My wife is waiting for me," he said.

"Liar," she said.

He took a few steps.

"You are leaving me here? I don't know the way back."
"Come, then."
"Oh, but you are cruel."

Perhaps he was cruel, and a fool, Giacomo thought that night, after his wife had left him as usual to go to her own room, near the children, on the second floor. He paced the hall, the drawing room, the corridors, the stairs. It wasn't long before he met Leonora. A glance, and she knew, as he knew, that he would be upstairs with her soon. He knocked at her bedroom door and found her waiting for him in her nightgown. But he was right—it wasn't love she met him with but greed. And insults. "You are a pig," she kept saying by way of endearment, when any normal person would have said "darling" or some other tender word. Could this be called love, for God's sake? When it was over, and he returned to his own room downstairs, he felt absolutely miserable. Never again, he thought, and though she stayed another two or three days, he kept his pledge. It was easy. Not that she stopped pursuing him. "Are you afraid of me?" she asked in a taunting voice. "What are you afraid of? Are you still afraid I'm going to eat you up?"

"Yes," he repeated.

Finally, she left for Ischia, but she continued to proclaim her love with long-distance calls and cards and letters that he didn't care about answering. Even when he went back with his family to America, where he had a home and where that year he was going to be artist in residence at a distant university, he didn't feel free of her. "I'm going to come and see you," she had told him. "What do you think? That I don't have money? I have plenty of money. Will you be alone? I think you ought to live alone when you go and teach."

Her cards kept coming, and for Christmas, by registered mail, so that he had to go to the town's main post office for it, a lovers' calendar full of jokes that didn't make him laugh, and gratuitous advice, and ugly pictures of bleeding hearts. With some misgiving, he dropped it in the trash bin.

A year later, he was back in Italy—alone this time. He had come because the house there was about to be sold. The huge, sprawling country house where he had grown up, whose every cranny he knew from cellar to attic, and the secret passages—even the pitted bricks—for sale! The house some of whose walls his mother had frescoed. The house his grandfather and mother and father had died in. The house where they had all laughed and loved, where he and his brothers had brought their laughing brides and entertained and danced; the house that had been the center of the most animated discussions (discussions that you had the illusion brought you close to the core of every subject broached), where friends lingered around the dinner table to hear his mother talk; the house that had resounded with poetry, read and recited, with the tapping of typewriters—his father at work on philosophy, his mother on translating (to pay some of the bills), his brother on ancient Greek; the house with his studio and the smell of paint, the smell of new wine, of peaches, grain, and olive oil, of firewood from the kitchen hearth. For sale. He could hardly believe it, yet a buyer had already made a down payment, and signs of the coming sale were almost everywhere.

Giacomo had come from America on a three-week charter flight and with a Eurailpass. Restless and wanting to see parts of Europe he had never been to, for two weeks he had travelled almost continuously, in Scandinavia

crossing the Arctic Circle, going as far north as the railroad allowed. The Eurailpass was an incentive to keep
moving—like having distance in his hands, something to
unravel the railroad network with. Athirst for distance, he
had gone on and on, never stopping in a hotel more than
one night, often sleeping on the train, stretched out on the
seats of half-empty carriages, feeling out of place in first
class, which the pass provided for, until, tired, sated, he
had come to his old house as to a haven, to sign a few
documents, choose some furniture, but mostly to savor a
last few days in it before it would belong to someone else.

He had found it in a pitiful state, looking like a depot
—all the good furniture and paintings moved into the
dining room and hall; the bedrooms bare; every wall
showing nail holes and lines left by tables, bureaus, and
bookshelves, and rectangular patches where paintings
and mirrors had hung. The house was no place to stay in,
and he spent as much time as he could out in the garden,
even having his meals there. The garden, apart from being
a little untended and overgrown, hadn't changed. The
house looked dead, or nearly so; in contrast, the plants
and trees were very much alive, and a comfort to his sight.
Those immense pines that the west wind had given a
permanent curvature at the top were his brothers. Those
cypresses—he had climbed them all, found bedlike resting places in the tufted foliage that, at various levels, had
collected. He knew them well, and in their company, with
a bottle of wine on the table, and bread and cheese and
fruit, he was quite happy. Silent companions, except for
the birds that perched or nested in them, and for the wind,
which made a soft and pleasing summer sound.

Back of the house, across a courtyard with three huge
walnut trees his father had planted forty years before,
there was another house—small, this one, and modest—

which also belonged to the family. In the old days, a good part of the downstairs had housed chickens, but a section with a big earthen tub and a stove was used as a laundry, where the linen was soaked in boiling water and potash, and another had a brick oven in which the bread was baked. Upstairs, a large room had held mats for silkworms; in another room grapes were hung to dry for a special wine. Over the years, the small house had been remodelled. Where the silkworms had munched mulberry leaves and coated themselves with glistening cocoons, now there was a studio. The laundry had been made into a pretty bedroom. There were three other rooms besides, and a little kitchen. The whole place was rented out to students; this summer, to some young Americans—four boys and two girls. Giacomo knew three of them. One, John, a graduate student in art history at Columbia, had stayed here with his wife three years before. They had separated, and now he was with a different girl—Sandra.

Giacomo first saw her from the doorway of the yard as she was drawing water from a faucet into a bucket full of clothes. Barefoot, bare-armed, barelegged, slim, sunburned, she had light-brown hair down almost to her waist. She wore the flimsiest clothes—blue, frayed at the thighs, and sunbleached. And on that hot July day he immediately got a sense of freshness seeing her, a girl in her early twenties washing her own clothes. He couldn't keep on looking without embarrassing her and he turned away, but the image of freshness lingered. In his mind that miserable faucet took on the aspect of a wonderful fountain. He wished he, too, were staying in the little house. Though he hadn't, on this visit, been inside, it must be almost unchanged. No look of a depot there. He returned to his own—the grand and now crippled, confused home.

Every room a mess. Even the kitchen. Piles of un-washed dishes. A sink full of them. The dishwasher out of order, just taking up space. Stove spattered with sauce. Fireplace a heap of ashes, papers burned and unburned. He felt like cleaning up. But why? His sister, who was in the house with her daughter, had got the dishes dirty and would wash only one or two for the next meal, leaving the rest undone. She wasn't bothered by anything like this. She was—here, at least—used to having things done for her. But now there was no one to do them. Unless it was he. Oh well. He rolled his shirt-sleeves up and did the dishes and cleaned the stove. But he didn't cook. This day and the subsequent ones, he just took some bread, cheese, and wine out of the pantry. His sister cooked plate-size steaks. She had suffered from consumption long ago and still considered them essential, both for herself and for her daughter. They, too, would have lunch in the garden.

As long as no harsh topics, like the division of property or past quarrels, were brought up, his sister's company was acceptable and even welcome. Her conversation and silence both had such casualness about them that it was soothing. She could be quite entertaining, too—tell a story quickly and make you laugh. She was absolutely informal, a gypsy born. One could see it at a glance from the way she dressed—a shawl wrapped around her waist in lieu of a skirt, a shawl over her breasts rather than a blouse; and from the way she sat—usually stretched out on a bench here by the garden table; and from the way she ate—ravenously. And still she had a certain charm that made children and younger people like her. In a way, she herself, though nearly forty, was still a child.

So they were eating in peace today, in the shade of an ilex, with the strong sun, only a few feet away, searing the grass, ripening the lemons, intensifying everything around. He was thinking of when his sister was small, of when they had all loved her, back to the time she was born, when she had seemed to be heaven-sent, a gift to the household, which till then had been too much the scurrying ground of three young boys. Yes, it was good to be here now alone with his sister and her daughter, at peace for once. And then she said, "Leonora may be coming today," and it was like a cloud crossing the blue sky.

"Really?" he said apprehensively.

"Yes. Why, aren't you glad? She's good company."

"I could do without it."

"Oh, she has a heart of gold."

He sighed and hung on to the hope in the word "may." But soon he heard the rumble of a car, and his sister said, "They have arrived."

"There's more than one?"

"She's coming with another woman."

His sister and her daughter went to the front door. He stayed where he was, and shortly he heard Leonora, as she stepped into the garden, say, *"Dov'è il mio amore?"*

She spotted him soon enough through the potted lemon trees, and she and her friend Magda—a middle-aged woman like herself, but one who struck you at once as having fewer pretensions as to looks and age, and a bit more sense—came over. They hadn't had lunch and were very hungry, Leonora said. She let herself drop down on a wicker chair and bounced up with a scream. She had sat on a little nail.

"Look! Look!" she said, turning around and drawing up her dress and slip to show them her bottom. "Blood!" And when they saw nothing she went on, "What pain!," though the pain by now must surely have abated. "Kill me you want to? Oh, God," and she hopped around as though she had been scalded. She stopped only when his sister brought her and Magda a steak-filled platter. They ate like ogres. "All the blood I lost," Leonora said. "Who knows how many corpuscles that nail took from me? I *need* this steak. Thank you, Clara."

Her vulgarity distressed him. In the presence of his mother and father, no one would have talked like that. They had always lent the house a dignity that now obviously was lacking.

Magda seemed to be there only to corroborate any statement Leonora made, laugh at her jokes, and praise her.

"Why didn't you answer my cards?" Leonora asked him.

"I answered one or two. Cards aren't like letters."

"And the calendar I sent you?"

"Oh, yes, thank you for the calendar," he said.

"You didn't acknowledge that."

"I lost your address."

"But it was on the envelope."

"I must have mislaid it," he said, the trash bin in his mind.

Magda looked at her. Had Leonora come all the way down here to see such a lacklustre, funless individual?

"You don't love me," Leonora said.

"I love my wife." Convenient to have a wife, for once, he thought.

"I don't like your wife," she said.

A man's ties with his wife might be strained to the point of divorce and still he would resent anything said against her. He became even quieter, and Leonora apologized. "Are you offended?" she said.

"No," he said weakly. So let her believe that he was hurt—put distance between them. In a little while, he left the table. From the house he heard the three women talking, laughing, screaming. No one missed him.

Perhaps he was being puritanical and rude, he thought. Perhaps he was wrong about her. Perhaps she was not so bad, not half as bad as he. He sighed. In the evening, he would try to be more friendly. Certainly anyone who loved was in a superior position to one who did not. If she would only leave him alone. What was he to do? He had submitted once. He would not submit again. But he might be polite.

"I love especially men like you who play hard to get," she told him that afternoon.

"I'm not playing."

"You don't want to play with me? Why don't you want to play with me?"

If it only were just playing, he would not refuse, he thought. But love was no game.

"Come on," she said. "Let's go for a walk."

He shook his head and laughed at man's and woman's roles so curiously reversed. "You make me feel like a fool," he said.

"You are a fool."

"Yes, let's leave it at that."

But she wouldn't. "You know that I'm irresistible at night," she said, and walked away, crooning, at a fast, almost military pace.

"Shall we go out to dinner?" Leonora said as evening came.

He wished he could be by himself. He wanted his last days at the house to be days of collection, concentration, peace. He remembered feeling the same way once before —returning to England from Canada in 1945. In 1940, he and his family were in England as refugees. On Italy's entry into the war, being sixteen, Italian, and technically an enemy alien, he was picked up at his boarding school, interned and shipped to Canada, where, after a year in a camp, he was released and finished school and college. At the end of the war, he had gone back to England on a freighter that had eleven other passengers aboard. They were sailing up the Mersey River to Manchester when the ship had to stop because of fog, and the passengers all went ashore to have a drink in a pub near the river. They wanted him to join them, but he went off for a long walk alone. There was so much to think about, so much to go over; the return was like meeting an old friend again— why should the passengers come between them? For five long years while he was away, he had thought of England, embattled, besieged and then besieging, finally invading those who would have invaded her. Let the reunion be a private, intimate affair. Now, too, his desire was to be left undisturbed to think about the past. But there was no food left in the house, and he didn't have a car and they did, and he didn't want to behave like a child who had to be coaxed. So he replied, "Yes, let's all go out to dinner."

Mario—his sister's boyfriend, a fairly old fellow—had arrived, and after a quarrel with Clara (the two were always quarrelling and making up: she had driven off in her car, with him following her in his, in a strange chase this way and that for miles) they finally all ended up in a restaurant halfway into town.

The place was rustic—a general country store, with a restaurant attached that in the summer had tables, under some locusts, in a yard shielded from the road by a low wall. The six of them sat at a large wooden table. A teen-age girl—the daughter of the owner—brought a white cloth, glasses, and bread and wine. They ordered pasta, which was long in coming, but it was nice here under the trees, with the breeze blowing, the stars shining, and the young moon leaning at an odd angle as though she might tip over like a rocking chair. And the evening became even nicer when, partway through the meal, Sandra and John came up the road on the other side of the low wall. Giacomo had that strange and yet familiar feeling you get when things you wish to happen become true. He and his sister and his sister's daughter waved to them to come over, which they did. And there she was, the girl he had seen looking fresher than the water she was drawing, and clearer.

John said they had come for a drink. Giacomo ordered more wine for everybody. Their presence fanned the conversation, so that people from other tables darted curious glances at them. A big, burly, unwieldy, dressed-up man stared at Leonora, seemed quite taken with her, and, attracted by her antics, ventured over and declared his admiration.

She disdained him. "I love *him*," she said, pointing at Giacomo. But the man wasn't put off. In hope and wonder, he continued looking at her.

They left, Giacomo buying six bottles of *spumante* to have at home. There, the four other young Americans from the small house joined them in the drawing room, which still had a few chairs. One by one, the bottles were uncorked.

It seemed Leonora's evening. She laughed wantonly, and, if auras exist, hers must have glowed. John, no less than the man at the restaurant, seemed drawn to her. "Who is she? Tell me about her," he said to Giacomo.

"An odalisque," Giacomo said.

" 'Odalisque,' " John repeated, savoring the word and, perhaps seeing a Matisse in his art historian's mind, went to sit beside her. Fascinated, he started talking to her with abandon and desire and expectation of desire fulfilled. And Sandra saw it and withdrew from him and went to sit next to Giacomo on the floor.

He felt her presence near him as a blessing. He didn't

question the motive. One doesn't—not when the favor is so graciously bestowed. And again he had the uncanny feeling of things taking the shape that he wished for them. He told her all he felt about her from the first moment he had seen her to the present; told her how dull, what an intolerable bore everything and everyone seemed to him compared to her; and how she had turned a tap into a spring, a bucket into a fountain. She took his hand and held it, and as he spoke to her she looked at him fixedly, seriously. And then she said what no one had ever said that way to him before: "Let's go." He rose and went toward the door. He felt the eyes of the others on him, but he didn't care what anybody thought. She followed him to the door. He took her hand. The corridor was dark. Oh, but he knew the way. She belonged to a blithe, spontaneous world that he knew little of. She led him there as surely as he led her up the stairs. Into his room they went —the same one Leonora had stayed in the year before.

For two days, Giacomo and Sandra didn't meet. He spent them storing and packing books, furniture, and paintings. Leonora and Magda left. Then Sandra and her friends and he went for an evening picnic in a wood. In a clearing, after the meal, they recited poems and improvised. It was fun, but it could hardly match the other night.

The next afternoon, the last whole day for him here— a day in which the house and the garden and the yards seemed deserted—he went for a short walk around a little orchard near the house, and there she was, all alone, sitting under an apricot tree on a height overlooking the fields west of the house. The wind was quite strong, making leaves and grass glisten in the clean bright air, blowing her hair and making it also glisten. She sat pensively and for a moment didn't see him coming, then she said, "Hi."

"This is one of my favorite spots, too," he said.

"It's the most beautiful place I've ever been in," she said.

"With you here, it is."

She smiled. "You are going tomorrow?"

"Yes. I wish I weren't now. Where are the others?"

"They've all gone into town."

"My sister and her friends left yesterday. We have the whole place to ourselves."

"Would you like an apricot?" she said, and rose and picked one for him.

"Are they having dinner in town?"

"Yes."

"You didn't want to go with them?"

"No. I've broken with John. We're still friends, but I sleep alone in a room of my own. Sex for him was just play." Her voice surprised him with its resonance.

"You are wise."

Eating the apricot, he lay down and looked at her. "This place," he said, "it has never seemed so beautiful to me as it does today; it has never been so good to me. Shall we have supper together, you and I? I've got some cheese and a bottle of good wine."

"Yes," she said. "Come to my house. I wish you weren't going."

"I hope to see you in New York this fall."

His elder brother had always liked the little house best; it was more homey, without pretenses—exposed beams on every ceiling, small windows that gave more depth to the view. There, that last evening, they ate at a little table she set, putting together her food and his.

"It's my best supper ever. Strange, isn't it, that my last days should also be the best—better even than those here with my mother and father or with my wife and children or anybody else? And so much better than being alone. . . ." He stopped. God, there was certainly no need of talking.

The summer breezes entered the room from windows on three sides. He had wanted peace, time to collect himself, time to remember. *This* was peace, this the silence that he wanted, a silence that soon she would not break but thread with her own voice—a silence, he thought, like that in between notes of music.

Run to the Waterfall

EXCEPT that a pretty woman—even if I were only to see her picture on a stray piece of paper I might find—would throw me into confusion and send me scurrying back into the city, I would have been a hermit. All the same, I am enough of one to seek a wood for company and for comfort. In grief and in despair, it is a wood that I resort to. Sometimes one needs to hide—to hide without being cramped, to hide in freedom—and nothing but a wood will do. I don't feel alone if there are trees. In their company, I feel that perhaps there is no more intelligent creation on this earth. A wood is my delight. I will not miss one if I can help it. Ten years ago, in San Francisco, I missed seeing Muir Woods, and, ever since, I have been wanting to return. Perhaps this was the reason that some months ago, in Puerto Rico, I was so determined not to miss the Caribbean National Forest.

My wife and little girl and I had stopped between planes at the airport of San Juan. I kept looking at my guidebook. It said the forest was one of the few tropical rain forests in the world. "Rain forest"—the very term intrigued me. I could almost hear the sound of the raindrops falling on leaves, each drop moving each leaf. "Let's stop over for a day," I said to my wife.

"Oh, we'll be coming back this way sometime again."

"We may never."

"Oh, yes, we will."

"No," I said, and thought of Muir Woods and San Francisco. "It's such a long way."

There we were, with five suitcases and as many paper bags, which we hadn't been able to check through. I stuffed them into lockers. We rented a blue car and drove away.

We saw Luquillo Beach, with its myriad palm trees, then turned inland and soon began to climb out of the strong heat, the fields of sugarcane, the palms and the bananas, up into a cloudy, misty, foggy region in which masses of vapor swept the ground and, thinning, sometimes disclosed the green of the rain forest. Now and then the rain wet the windshield like soft, huge drops of dew. Soon we reached a clearer region. Here, rising above the general level of the forest, were trees with a silvery-white shimmering of leaves. One of these leaves—enormous, green, and long-stemmed—dropped on the hood of our car, then flapped over against the windshield on its silvery underside.

An intricacy of leaves of giant ferns lined the road like a green and living finely chiselled wall. And there were various flowers, and not bamboos but what seemed enlargements of bamboos, five or six times their usual size. Here we stopped and got out of the car. Down in the valley or by the sea there were a thousand noises. Not up here. Here a silent life had asserted itself and taken hold, and we stood silent amid the silent trees. Sometimes one bamboo knocked against another, making a weird tap, accentuating the silence and the stillness.

It began raining, not with hard, pelting drops but gently, in a way the most delicate blossom would enjoy. Farther up, close to the mountain crest, we came to a resort where we hoped to spend the night. It was quite hidden from the road, but a sign said, "Rain Entrance to the Restaurant." This was down a flight of steps—a large, stone structure with a terrace built over a deep gully. At the bottom of the gully, a stream rushed down the mountain between rocks. The cabins were a few minutes' walk away, isolated and hidden in the deep, luxuriant wood. Two botanists, husband and wife, ran the place. There was about them something quite familiar—perhaps the courtesy of an earlier generation. After we had eaten, they provided us with an electric stove, a flashlight, and a few books—one of them a guide to the Caribbean I had long been looking for. In the pitch-black night, with the baby in my arms and my wife a little scared, taking tiny steps, we advanced down a path I had been shown through wet, high foliage, into the wood, down to a cabin. Below, we could hear the stream rushing in the gully. I turned the key. The door, swollen by dampness, wouldn't open. My wife sighed. The night seemed even darker than it was. Big splashing drops dripped on us from the roof and from the trees, so different from raindrops, hitting us in the most vulnerable spots—the nape of the neck, the back of the hands, the nose, and the forehead. But when, after a violent push, the door did open, and I had switched the lights on and shut the door behind us and lit the stove, we felt snug, in fairyland. I couldn't help going out again to take a look at our little house all lighted up in the middle of the woods.

In the morning, after breakfast, I noticed a sign by the restaurant that said "To the Waterfall." I inquired how far it was.

"Half an hour's walk each way," the host replied.

Our airplane left at noon, and I figured it was an hour-and-a-half drive to the airport. It was past nine-thirty now. Could I make it to the waterfall? Not if I took an hour. "I'll be back in twenty minutes," I said, and rushed away.

I ran down a twisting, narrow path over slippery wet rocks and jagged stones down to the stream, and then across it and along it. As though someone were chasing me, I ran, raced, jumped down the craggy path, and in ten minutes began to hear the waterfall. Then the path suddenly became very steep. I took it like a boy rushing down a staircase out of school, and reached the pool at the bottom of the fall.

It seemed like a resounding triumph, that water falling without break, perennial, fed as much from the earth as from the sky. No question of a drought up on this mountain. Here it rained daily. The plants were as sure of getting water as was the seaweed with the rising of the tide.

I hurried back, taking twice the time it took me to come down. My wife and daughter were waiting for me near the car. As I looked at them, flushed and recovering my breath, I felt so much like a boy it seemed strange to have a wife and child there waiting for me. Even the car looked strange—could I be old enough to have a driver's license? Perhaps I would never feel so young again. That run to the waterfall had shaken off my shoulders more than twenty years.

Our hosts were by the car, insisting that we go back to San Juan the way we had come, that we would never make it if we went on, as I had intended to, over the mountain crest and down the other side. Reluctantly—I believed we had the time—I took their advice. I turned the car around, and immediately I felt old again. Thirty-nine. Past thirty-nine.

A Place in Italy

THE place exists. I see it, high over the valley, one of the highest points on the horizon—a jagged relevance, blue in the distance. We are in the car, going away from it, about ten miles off. I catch one last glimpse of it. Then it is gone.

"No, it isn't practical for you," the architect's wife says —as if that would cross it out of my mind forever. But it won't be crossed out. I continue to see it, though it is no longer in view. "It's beautiful, but it's not practical," she says, and the others agree. The architect himself, who is driving, has already had his say. He didn't approve of it, said that it should cost only half as much as it did, and that the extensive repairs it needed would double its price. In short, he made me feel as though I had flunked an exam. But the place keeps smiling to me, as though we had a secret entente, as though it were a new friend whom all my old ones were critical of, but whom, despite their adverse criticism, I continued to like. I like it more and more.

Even the children didn't take to it, the way I thought they would. I expected them to be on my side, to stare at it with marvel in their eyes, and shout, "Oh, let's buy it, Daddy." But they didn't. The little girl was feeling carsick from the many turns in the road going up to it, and the little boy was overwhelmed by the tall grass, the sheer loneliness of it. As for my wife, she said exactly what I might have foreseen she would say: "Someone's gone to the bathroom there." Those were her first words. I laughed to myself—there were no bathrooms, but what she saw plainly wasn't of human origin, and, glancing to one side, I saw a flock of sheep huddled against a wall, afraid of us. "It's the sheep," the architect's wife said to her sternly. My older girl wasn't there. I wonder what she would have thought of it.

Coming up to it, we had left the country road for a narrow, stony, curving track that led up around the steep, wooded hill to the house. Halfway up, we had to stop for a small tree that had fallen across the way. "Let's just leave the car here and walk," the architect said, and so we did. "Smell the broom, the *ginestra,*" I said, elated to get out of the car. It was May, the sun hot, and the heat seemed to express from the flowers all of their scent and disperse it in the warm air. I took great breaths of it and started up the little road, hardly able to walk, because in my eagerness I felt an urge to run. But I contained my enthusiasm, and kept at only a short distance ahead of the others.

"Are you sure this is the right road?" my wife said.

"Yes, of course."

I had been there a few weeks before with a real-estate man from Orvieto, a kindly old fellow with a sparse gray mustache, a pipe, a narrow-brimmed soft sage-green hat, and a pair of binoculars—a handy thing for him to have, given the setting of the place. Orvieto is perhaps the most unusual town in Italy after Venice, being built high over the plain on a table mountain, an Italian mesa. The cliffs on all sides make it impregnable, or almost. A town with an aerial feel, it has been pictured as standing on the palm of a hand raised over the valley. A small town—about thirty thousand people—with an immense cathedral, possibly the finest in the country. The other buildings are of gray stone or brown tufa; the sides of the cathedral are striped like a zebra with white and black marble. Its windows are of stained glass or thin, transparent alabaster, and much of the façade is finely carved or laden with mosaics. One has the impression of having come upon an outsized jewel among the common stones. The town has a very large number of palaces and churches for its size, and—so that the people wouldn't go thirsty in case of siege, when the Roman aqueduct that fed it could be easily cut off—a well that is at least as deep as the cliffs around the town are high. Dug into the tufaceous rock, it has two spiral stairways down around the shaft. There is an old saying that if you looked up at the sky at twilight from the bottom, you could see the stars before you could see them from the surface.

Coming to the south edge of the town, the real-estate man showed me, through the binoculars, two farmhouses in the distance. Without having to go there, I decided they weren't for me. Not unusual enough, too close to a road.

"I'll take you to a farmhouse with a tower, near Castel Viscardo," he said.

On the way, we stopped at an old house he had bought for himself. It was set on a rocky mound, once an Etruscan burial ground. The outlines of some of the tombs, opened and filled in again, were still visible in the tufa. He said he was an amateur sculptor, and planned to carve the rocks, leaving them in place. I wondered if their original form could be improved upon. From his house we went to "mine." Rain was threatening. The sky was leaden and silver. It was near sunset. There was a strange light—eerie, ecliptic. And though the sky was overcast, the clouds were high, the visibility quite good. We went up the little road through the wood. The way was clear then; the tree hadn't fallen. Beyond the wood we came to a grove of olive trees that hadn't been pruned for a long time and had a wild, untended look, then to a row of mulberry and cherry trees leading up to the house. This was even better than his, I thought—grander, higher, more isolated. On the right was the old tower, of stone and with a roof. It had a beautiful arched doorway, framed, like the windows, by slabs of a darker, gray-blue stone. The door was locked and he didn't have the key. But, going round the back, I found that a ground-floor window gave when I pushed it, and we both clambered through. The room, empty of all furniture, had a large stone fireplace and an inviting stairway up. This branched—one branch led to the house and its two bedrooms, the other to the second and third, or top, floor of the tower. The room on the top floor was under the rafters of the roof. One of these was supported by a pole. The room had no windows, only narrow openings at each corner, and, set into the walls, many round, widemouthed, empty earthen vases—nests for pigeons. There were no pigeons anymore. The place had been uninhabited for years. On the ground floor of the house were two stables, one with a long and handsome terra-cotta manger. At a right angle to them were more stables and barns and a porch. There, under the porch roof, I saw for a moment a table, set, with family and friends around it, wine on the table, a white tablecloth . . . a scene out of the past, or in the future? Desperately I wished that it might come to be. Dug into the rock of the steep slope some fifty feet back of the house was the wine cellar. You had the feeling that on a very clear day you could see for a hundred miles in all directions—a vast, almost limitless view of dawn and sunset. Below, to the east, a river valley; to the west, ridges, ranges, woods. And here and there in the wide landscape a distant village, a castle, an isolated farmhouse. Orvieto, too, lay below, eight miles away. Nearer, the roofs of the old village of Castel Viscardo. Nothing ugly in sight. The house's steep hill, or mound, was really the highest point of a grassy ridge. The yard extended southward into a broad sweep of grass combed by the wind. It was Italy as it might have looked a hundred years ago, pastoral, bucolic. Yes, I was enthusiastic about the place. That the roofs and some of the walls, doors, and windows needed extensive repairs, that there was no running water or bathrooms, that the electric wiring would all have to be redone meant little to me. There was a spring nearby. I would build an aqueduct. I had always wanted to build one. I would get a mason and a carpenter to come and help me with the repairs, perhaps give work to someone unemployed. I would get to know the villagers this way. For a moment nothing daunted me. "Yes, I would like to buy it," I said. "I like it. I like it very much."

"It certainly is an original place," he said.

"Yes. My family had a country house near Siena which, unfortunately, we sold three years ago, after my parents died. It was a foolish thing to do, and I constantly regret it. This place would make up for it in part. It has some of its good qualities and none of its defects. Oh, I wouldn't live here all the time. Maybe a few months a year. I live in America, but I am free—I paint—and I would come. Do you think it might be broken into while I was away?"

He tilted his head, not in a nod or a denial but as if to say that it could happen. "The worst are the hunters," he said. "You'd have to get someone to keep an eye on it. One of these shepherds maybe. And put a fence around it."

No, not a fence, I thought. It would interrupt the sweep of the landscape. But a neighbor to look after it, yes.

"Well, I'd certainly like to buy it, but first I'll have to

show it to my wife," I said. And I left in buoyant spirits.

All the way to Rome, I felt euphoric, the way one feels when one has discovered something after a long search. Why, I thought, the place was so beautiful one would want to travel miles to see it, come and watch the sunset from it, have a picnic at the foot of the old tower under the cherry and olive trees. I could see myself returning with the car, the children cheering, and, all at the same time, the cherries ripe, friends sitting at the dinner table, the stables made into comfortable rooms, the fireplace in the tower lit, paintings and books around me, and music, the top room and every other room furnished, the garden blossoming. Yet no major changes made in the structure of the place, nothing demolished or torn down, everything left standing.

But it wasn't to be. Impractical. "I want to buy it," I tell my wife again and again, and she replies, "All right, go ahead, but you'll never get me there."

And I haven't the heart to do it alone. What is property to me anyway? Can you really own a piece of land, a house? Aren't we all sojourners, tenants in this world? And yet the place attracts me. I am almost on the point of going to Orvieto with my checkbook. The world is mine. I am in the driver's seat. But only for a moment. The words ring in my ear: "you'll never get me there." And I withdraw to my room and slump on the bed and pull the bedspread over my head and lie still as a mummy until, short of air, I am forced to uncover my nose.

We have some money in the bank—the sale of the old family house. Inflation bites into it. The lira dips. We should invest it somehow. We've seen dozens of houses and apartments, and inquired about a hundred more. In this year in which I am in Italy, that's all I seem to do. But in Rome, where we are staying, what's for sale is either too expensive or too small, and none of the places we've seen outside of Rome can compare with that one near Orvieto. Oh, yes, there was a place on the Argentario I took my wife to. It had a full view of the sea, of the island of Giglio, of Montecristo, even of Corsica on the clearest days, but she said it was too small, and it wasn't a whole house, just a half house. It had its own garden, though, lemon trees, a portico. There was an old mill, too, between Pisa and Lucca, that we went to see. But that was too large, needed too much work, the view wasn't to her liking. She has seen several one- or two-room apartments in Rome. These you could rent, she says. But we could never live in one—not the five of us, I say. And so the weeks pass and the months, and our stay in Italy is almost at an end. But I won't give up.

On weekends I sally forth into the country, sometimes alone, sometimes with wife and children. Besides the places mentioned, I have been to Venice, Florence, Narni, Todi, Spoleto, the Circeo, the mountains of Tolfa, Subiaco, the Sabine Mountains, Viterbo, Arezzo, Bagnaia, Lake Trasimeno, San Gimignano, Bolsena. I have seen places I would never have seen otherwise, and met some unusual people in the process. In the Sabine Mountains, a parish priest, and real-estate agent in his spare time, showed us, among other things, what he described as a "terrific" buy—a onetime convent that was now an abandoned ruin. The cracks in the walls were indeed terrific; there were floors missing; through the roof not only would it rain in but you would see the stars. Might as well try to restore the Colosseum. In Subiaco, I saw a tiny house, unreachable by car, a tremendous walk from the main street. Perhaps when I was young. . . . Near Lake Trasimeno, I was shown an old farmhouse, fully restored, well worth its price. But every tile, door, window, step spoke out the owner's taste—it would remain his even after I had finished paying for it. Yet by going to see it I came across the pretty town of Panicale. On its outskirts there is the little Church of St. Sebastian. It was closed, but a boy came to unlock the door for me, and there, at one end, taking up the whole wall, was Perugino's fresco "The Martyrdom of St. Sebastian"—the calm faces of the archers and of the saint, the faded gentle colors, the serene Umbrian countryside. In Spoleto, a real-estate lady who quoted Leopardi and Horace showed me around. Near the Lake of Bolsena, a count drove me down an incredibly steep road in the woods to a little farmhouse he wanted to sell. The farmer and his wife were there. The man was ill, and told us his sad story. Toward the end of our visit, the wife went to get a bottle of wine from their cave cellar. She uncorked it. It fizzed almost like champagne, and like champagne it was light and very dry—and cold, having been "cool'd a long age in the deep-delvèd earth." In Bagnaia, it was market day, and a comedy atmosphere pervaded the little town. In the main square, I felt as if I were on a stage, an actor among actors, all perfectly unaware.

And still no house.

We have only ten days before we have to board a plane for Boston. It seems too late to try to buy anything now. A friend says, "It's mad for you to leave your money in the bank."

Money in the bank. In my youth, we were always short of money—lots of land, a big house, but very little cash. Therefore, keeping money in the bank doesn't seem mad to me. Not mad to have ready access to it, especially since I have no job, no salary, but only do free-lance work. But another consideration makes me go on one last errand for a house: I don't want to leave Italy without owning something in it, a place to repair to in case hotels and the houses of friends and relatives should suddenly all seem inhospitable to me, a place where I can leave a few of my things—some of my books, a desk, a chair, a bed, pots and pans and dishes, something familiar to return to. And so I rent a car and venture out again, in my pocket an address from a classified ad in the *Messaggero*. It's one that I saw weeks ago but ignored because the price seemed ridiculously low: twenty-three hundred dollars. A barn, I thought, or storeroom—no place that I could live in. But on the telephone I asked if it might be suitable as a studio, and the man said yes, it was, and he gave me good directions and the name of the caretaker. "His real name," he said, "is Anselmo Remi, but you'd better ask for Cimitella or you won't find him. Everyone knows him as Cimitella."

I follow the Autostrada del Sole up the Tiber Valley toward Orte. Here the Tiber isn't tawny, as in Rome, but green-blue. I know the valley well. Up to the right in the fields, below a hamlet, I see what from the road seems a speck but is a little farmhouse that an English writer friend of mine bought long ago. I am sure he is there typing, while his Italian wife is quietly painting in the room below. I won't go to see them this trip. I have no time. I go on up the river ten more miles, take a left, follow a stream along its gorge, then gradually drive up a craggy hillside. It's good to leave the expressway and be here on this curving, narrow road. I feel at home amid the olives and the vines. Up high, on top of a hill, across the stream, is a cluster of stone houses the color of the rocks below. Everything blends delightfully. It is the hand of time that makes it so. My village is the next one, on this side of the stream, and higher than that one. I come to the first houses and then to a central little square.

"Where can I find Cimitella?" I ask.

"Ah, Cimitella? Eh, you go up there, up to the very top, beyond the arch."

On up I drive. Just before the arch the road bends so sharply that my car, though it is a small Fiat, gets by only after some maneuvering. On my right I skirt a wall below which is a sheer drop, and I come to another square and a church and a castle. Here I leave the car and ask for Cimitella again. Somebody smiles and directs me higher still. I go up a lane in a zigzag. A bunch of small children peek and hide behind a corner and laugh uproariously. A dog barks playfully. I come to Cimitella's house. Everything is little here, except the castle and the church. Cimitella's wife—a pleasant, smiling, middle-aged woman— appears at the doorway, and calls her husband for me. He's talking to some neighbors in a lane. Spare, with an expressive, friendly face and bright eyes, he comes over, and down we go to see the "studio." It turns out that it's on the first little square I stopped at on arriving. The studio is on the second floor of a small house that juts out into the square. It has a medieval aspect. It's made of stone. It has an outside staircase, and it is buttressed by two chimneys. It must be seven or eight hundred years old. Yet it's not dilapidated. Simply worn. The stone steps are hollowed out by use through the centuries. On top of the staircase is a little terrace. Cimitella unlocks the door. There is a room with a beautiful ancient fireplace, and another little room. It has running water and a light. From two of the windows you can see the countryside; another window looks onto the square. Yes, it's much better than I expected. And the floor below, too, is for sale, for less than the second—for about a thousand dollars—so that by buying both I can have a little house.

I return to Rome quite enthusiastic about my find. But

my wife won't go to see it. I am determined to buy it, though. And so, a few days before our departure, I sign a contract. Then I make one last visit to it, alone, for no one will come with me. I meet Cimitella again, and a mason. He is going to restore it for me—mend the floor and roof, put in a bathroom, replaster the inside walls. And I'll have our things moved in. Someday, I hope, my children will laugh with the children of the village, and my wife will sleep there with me. Nearby is Monte Cimino, and a lake, and the old town of Viterbo, and the villages on the tops of hills. Cimitella points them out: "Orte, Attigliano, Chia, Giove," he says. One of them is actually called Giove—Jupiter—and it is as if he were pointing at the planets and the stars, naming them one by one.